"Would you like to come to my house?"

Christopher asked Harris.

Julia, who'd just taken a drink of lemonade, nearly choked at her son's invitation. Her hand went to her throat, and she swallowed with difficulty.

Harris watched her, wondering if she would have had the same reaction if Christopher had invited some other man. He wondered what it was about him that Julia Warren didn't seem to like.

"I'd love to, but I'm afraid I can't today," he told the boy. "Maybe soon."

"Tomorrow?"

"Harris has to work, Christopher," Julia said, suddenly finding her voice.

Christopher's head sank dejectedly and Julia felt a pang. Her son was so hungry for male companionship.

And if she was honest with herself, so was she....

Dear Reader,

The festive season is often so hectic—a whirlwind of social calls, last-minute shopping, wrapping, baking, tree decorating and finding that perfect hiding place for the children's gifts! But it's also a time to pause and reflect on the true meaning of the holiday: love, peace and goodwill.

Silhouette Romance novels strive to bring the message of love all year round. Not just the special love between a man and woman, but the love for children, family and the community, in stories that capture the laughter, the tears and, *always,* the happy-ever-afters of romance.

I hope you enjoy this month's wonderful love stories—including our WRITTEN IN THE STARS selection, *Arc of the Arrow* by Rita Rainville. And in months to come, watch for Silhouette Romance titles by your all-time favorites, including Diana Palmer, Brittany Young and Annette Broadrick.

The authors and editors of Silhouette Romance books wish you and your loved ones the very best of the holiday season . . . and don't forget to hang the mistletoe!

Sincerely,

Valerie Susan Hayward
Senior Editor

STELLA BAGWELL

Done to Perfection

Silhouette Romance

Published by Silhouette Books New York

America's Publisher of Contemporary Romance

To all those seeking justice

SILHOUETTE BOOKS
300 E. 42nd St., New York, N.Y. 10017

DONE TO PERFECTION

ISBN: 0-373-08836-1

First Silhouette Books printing December 1991

Printed in the U.S.A.

Books by Stella Bagwell

Silhouette Romance

STELLA BAGWELL

lives with her husband and teenage son in southeastern Oklahoma, where she says the weather is extreme and the people friendly. When she isn't writing romances, she enjoys horse racing and touring the countryside on a motorcycle.

Stella is very proud to know that she can give joy to others through her books. And now, thanks to the Oklahoma Library for the Blind in Oklahoma City, she is able to reach an even bigger audience. The library has transcribed her novels onto cassette tapes so that blind people across the state can also enjoy them.

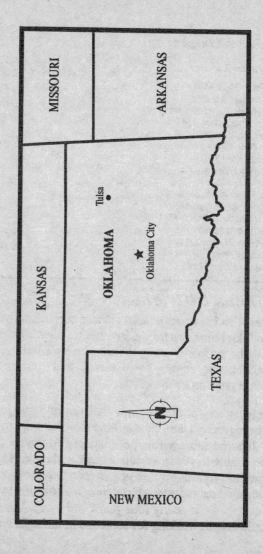

Chapter One

It was well after midnight and Julia Warren's face was lined with exhaustion as she slumped into a chair. With a weary sigh, she pushed the auburn hair away from her face and mumbled, "I don't want to do it. And even if I wanted to, I don't think I could."

"Did I hear you right?"

Julia glanced across the workroom at Rhonda, her friend and co-worker. "I'm afraid so."

The petite, dark-haired woman's expression showed concern as she tossed several crusty pots into a deep, stainless-steel sink filled with soapy water. "Does this have anything to do with the fact that the man is a judge?"

Julia propped her feet out in front of her and rubbed her throbbing temples. She and Rhonda had been in the catering business for three years now, and during that time they'd been through thick and thin together. "It's—I know it's been nearly four years, but I just don't think I could handle working for someone in the legal system."

Rhonda tried to sound persuasive. "The Hargroves are rich people, Julia. Just the sort we like to work for. They'll spare no expense."

Closing her eyes, Julia wished she was in bed. It had been a long day spent catering an outside fund-raiser for a local boys' club. The weather had been a scorching hundred plus as they'd served pounds of barbecue to the endless number of attendees. Every muscle in Julia's body was aching, and Rhonda's suggestion that they cater a party for Judge Harris T. Hargrove seemed to be making the pain worse.

"They might be rich, but they're also people of the law."

Rhonda turned away from the sink to face Julia. "I understand that, honey. But you have to let go of the past sometime. Carl's death was a terrible thing, but I hate to think of you harboring all that bitterness inside you forever. Besides, you were once connected to the legal system yourself."

Julia had heard these sorts of remarks from Rhonda before. They were well meaning, but for some reason they bothered Julia more than usual tonight. "I know. And I hate the fact that I can't change the way I feel. Believe me, I've tried."

Rhonda finished drying a pan, then stacked it aside with the others. "Well, I can certainly understand that. I'm still bitter about Bobby and our divorce. But that doesn't mean I'm down on all men."

Julia propped her chin on her fist and contemplated her friend's words. "So you're saying I shouldn't be down on all judges just because one allowed a criminal out on bail, thus giving him the chance to kill my husband?"

Rhonda's reply was guarded. "Something like that, I guess."

Frowning wryly, Julia again pushed her hair from her face. "That's easier said than done."

Rhonda walked across the room and put her hand on Julia's shoulder. "I understand, honey. Really I do. I only want you to consider this offer. In the long run our business would profit from it."

Under no circumstances could Julia imagine catering for a judge. It went against everything inside her. But Rhonda was her business partner and Julia couldn't simply ignore her wishes. "I won't make any promises," she said, "except that I'll think about it."

Rhonda smiled brightly and squeezed her friend's shoulder. "Thanks. That's all I ask."

Julia smiled tiredly back at her. "Let's forget this mess. We can finish in the morning," she suggested, gesturing at the dirty cooking utensils and vessels still strewn here and there on the counters. "I don't know about you, but I'm dog-tired."

"You go on in," Rhonda insisted. "I'm only going to finish this one last pot in the sink and then it's off to bed for me, too."

The two women exchanged good-nights and Julia slipped out the door. Outside, she rounded the garage-turned-workshop then passed through a small gate. The back door of her house was only some thirty feet away. As she headed across the lawn, she glanced up at the night sky. It was cloudless, but the humidity made the stars blurred and dim. Oklahoma City was always hot in June and would be even hotter in July.

It was one of the busiest times of the year for the catering business with the endless number of outdoor parties going on. Was there really a need to book the Hargrove party? she asked herself. Their calendar was already jammed.

With a tired groan, Julia stepped into the quiet house and made her way through the familiar darkness until she reached her son's bedroom. The baby-sitter had left the night-light on by the bed, bathing the tawny-headed child in a soft yellow glow.

Julia leaned down and brushed her fingers along his cheeks, then pushed the straight spikes of hair off his forehead. Fierce love and pride surged through her as her eyes traveled over his sleeping face. During the past four years she'd watched his features change from those of an infant to the more mature features of a little boy. She liked to think his long-lashed eyes and full lips resembled hers. But she had to concede that Chris's square jaws and snub nose closely resembled Carl's.

Thoughts of her late husband pulled her gaze to the small gold-framed picture on the bedside table. Carl, in his police uniform, smiled back. She kept the photo by Christopher's bed to assure the boy that at one time he'd had a father who'd adored his new baby son.

Glancing back down at Christopher, she realized the child was her life now. He was the reason she worked so hard at her catering business. He was the reason she'd pulled herself together after Carl's death and gone on with her life.

Her eyes misty, she leaned down and brushed a whisper-soft kiss against the boy's cheek, then straightened the sheet and tucked it securely around him.

Leaving the room, she crossed the hall to her own bedroom and quickly shed her jeans and T-shirt. In the adjoining bathroom, she adjusted the shower, then stepped into the enclosure. The cool spray felt wonderful against her tired muscles and for long minutes she simply stood there letting the water soak into her thick mane of hair and wash over her body.

Julia wished the shower could just as easily wash away the problem of Judge Hargrove's party. It was obvious that Rhonda wanted to take the job. And since it would be a rather large party, there was no way she could do it without Julia's help.

Rhonda had been her dearest friend for a long time. Even before she'd lost Carl. She could usually discuss anything with her, but this time, when Rhonda had mentioned their potential client was a judge, she'd felt something freeze inside her. She'd immediately wanted to drop the whole subject of doing a party for the man. But guilt had followed right behind those feelings, compelling Julia to promise Rhonda she'd think about it.

Damn it, she wished Judge Hargrove had never called their catering business in the first place. Then she wouldn't feel wedged between a rock and a hard place.

When Julia came out of the bathroom, the phone beside the bed was ringing. Wrapped in a white towel, she sat on the edge of the bed and lifted the receiver.

"Julia, were you already in bed?"

It was Rhonda. "No, I just got out of the shower. Is something wrong?"

Rhonda sighed heavily. "Not really. I'm just afraid I've upset you with this Hargrove deal. You know I'd never push you into anything you really didn't want to do."

Julia absently plucked at the towel. "I know, Rhonda. Don't worry about it."

Rhonda was silent for a moment, then said, "Oh, honey, I know how you're looking at things. But it wasn't a judge who killed Carl. It was a criminal. And it certainly wasn't Judge Harris T. Hargrove who let him out on bail."

Sighing ruefully, Julia closed her clear gray eyes. "I know you're right," she murmured. "But lately Carl seems to be in my thoughts more than ever. I don't know, Rhonda, but my life seems to be splintered in all directions."

"That's probably because you're still partly living in the past," Rhonda said gently.

"Maybe that's true, but then so are you..." Julia solemnly added, referring to Rhonda's lingering bitterness over her divorce.

Both women fell silent. After a few moments, Rhonda spoke. "Look, the way I see it, this birthday bash for Mrs. Hargrove will be a cleansing step for you, and I'll make it one for me, too."

"What do you mean?" Julia asked, lying on her side and propping herself on an elbow.

"If you can do a job for a judge, it will prove you can put Carl's tragedy behind you. And if you do that, surely it will give me the incentive to forget Bobby."

Julia rolled her eyes. "Catering one more party is going to make us forget the men in our past? I really doubt it, Rhonda."

"Don't be negative, Julia. At least it will be a start. Come on, say you'll do it," she pleaded.

Julia knew she was probably making a big mistake even before she spoke. "All right," she said with obvious reluctance. "I suppose it would be foolish not to take the man's money."

"Now you're talking, girl," Rhonda said happily. "I'll call him first thing in the morning and set the ball rolling."

Julia groaned. "I'm so tired right now I don't even want to think about morning."

"We have that small dinner party for the Gilmores' anniversary scheduled for tomorrow evening. But that's all. It's going to be an easy day." Rhonda yawned. "So I'm off to bed now."

"Good night, Rhonda."

"Night, honey."

Julia replaced the receiver then turned and rested her head against the pillows. Could Rhonda be right? she wondered. Would doing the party for Judge Hargrove be a step toward getting on with her own life?

She hardly thought so. It had been four years since the night Carl had been fatally shot by a person who, by all rights, should have been in jail. Time had not lessened her outrage, nor had it enabled her to come to grips with the utter senselessness of it all. And coming face-to-face with a judge was only going to remind her of how flawed the judicial system was, she thought grimly. But then, it wasn't written anywhere that she had to like her clients. Which was a good thing, because she already knew she didn't like Judge Harris T. Hargrove.

"Mommy, Mommy wake up! Josephine is on the light!"

Groaning, Julia forced one eye to open, then the other. Her son was standing by the side of her bed. "What are you saying, Chris?" she mumbled sleepily.

"It's Josephine. She's in the kitchen. On the light."

More awake now, Julia pushed herself up to a sitting position. "Chris, do you mean my new stained-glass lamp over the table?"

The small pajama-clad boy nodded anxiously and Julia gave him a reproving look. "Chris, what did I tell you about the door to the bird cage?"

Christopher ducked his head, then glanced sheepishly back up at his mother's stern expression. "You said not to open it. But she was hungry and—"

"Now she's out," Julia finished for her son, yet her voice held no harshness. At times like these she reminded herself what it was like to be four years old without a brother or sister for playful companionship. Christopher had pleaded for a dog, but Julia's yard wasn't properly fenced. She'd compromised with a parrot, and Christopher loved the bird. Sometimes too much.

"She flew past me, Mommy. I couldn't catch her and now she just sits on the light and squawks at me."

"Go see if she's still there, while Mommy finds her robe," Julia told him, reaching up and pushing the tangled hair from her face.

The boy raced out of the room before Julia had swung her feet to the floor.

"She's still here, Mommy," Chris shouted from the kitchen.

"Okay, honey, I'm coming." Julia found her thin cotton robe on a chair in the corner of her room and quickly wrapped it around her. By the time she reached the kitchen Chris had climbed onto the middle of the oak table. Just out of his reach was a large parrot who'd decided to use her stained glass swag lamp for a swing.

"You darn bird! Come down from there!" Julia held her finger out as a perch, but the bird ignored it.

"Chris! Chris!" Josephine squawked.

Julia let out a frustrated breath as she menacingly eyed the bird. "Get a cracker, Chris. Maybe she'll come down for that."

While Chris scampered down from the table to fetch the cracker, Julia continued to try to coax the parrot down from the lamp.

"Josephine, if you don't come down now I'm going to tell everyone that you're really a boy!" Julia threatened.

"Boy! Boy!" the parrot repeated.

"Here, Mommy! She'll come down to eat this." Chris handed his mother a cracker.

Julia took it and offered it up to the contrary bird. It took a bit of coaxing, but after a few minutes Julia got her hands on him. "Now, you naughty bird, it's back to the cage with you."

Chris scampered into the living room ahead of his mother and opened the door to the large cage. As Julia placed the bird back inside, the telephone began to ring. "Will you answer that please, Chris?" she asked as she latched the door behind the ruffled parrot. "Serves you right," she said to Josephine. "You know better than to get on my new lamp."

"It's Auntie Rhonda, Mommy," Chris announced, tossing down the receiver on the arm of the couch. "She wants to talk to you."

Julia turned away from the cage and crossed to the phone. The bird began squawking loudly.

"Hi, Rhonda," Julia said. "You up already?"

"What's the matter with Josephine?" Rhonda asked.

Julia groaned good-naturedly. "She escaped from her cage and I threatened to tell everyone she was a Joe instead of a Josephine."

Rhonda chuckled. "That's inhumane. It would ruin her image."

"*His* image," Julia corrected. The bird really was a he, but the pet store had somehow mislabeled its sex. It wasn't until they'd already named Josephine that the pet store called to inform her of the error.

"Don't confuse me this early in the morning," Rhonda pleaded with a moan. "I have troubles."

"What kind of troubles?" Julia sat down on the couch as she waited for her friend to elaborate.

"My tooth. I bit into a bagel and the filling came out."

"Oh, no! Is it hurting you?"

"It's killing me. I think a nerve's been exposed."

"Then you'd better see a dentist this morning if you can get an appointment," Julia insisted. "You shouldn't put off something like that. It might become abscessed."

"That's exactly what I thought. That's why I'm calling you. I should be back in plenty of time to help start the dinner for the Gilmores tonight. But you'll have to meet Judge Hargrove this morning at eleven."

"Wh-what?" Julia gasped.

"The party. He needs to talk with one or both of us about it. And since I can't go, you'll have to."

Julia gripped the telephone. "Call him back and tell him you'll come later."

"Julia! The man is a judge, for heaven's sake. He has to work around a heavy schedule."

Julia grimaced. "Well, so do I."

"Julia, please don't be difficult now! I'm in too much pain!"

Seeing no way out of this, Julia dropped her head and rubbed her forehead with her fingers. "He's probably some old crotchety thing who thinks he's God." All judges did, didn't they? she silently asked herself. "Don't blame me if I come home saying I lost my temper and blew the whole thing."

Rhonda clucked her tongue. "Don't think in those terms, Julia. Remember, this is a new beginning. You're simply going to see a client about a party."

"Some client," Julia muttered. "But all right, I'll do my best. Where do I see the man?"

Rhonda sighed with obvious relief. "At the courthouse. In his office."

Julia frowned. "I'm not crazy about going to the courthouse. The last time I was there I wanted to commit murder myself."

"Well, I suppose the man's too busy to meet you anywhere else. At any rate, that was then and this is now. Besides, you probably won't see him for more than five minutes. Just be sure to get the number of invited guests, complete menu, and see if he'd like any special decorations."

"Yes, I know. I'll write it all down. You go on and take care of that tooth."

"Can I trust you to be civil to the man?" Rhonda asked anxiously.

Julia frowned. "It'll be difficult, but I'll manage."

Rhonda said, "Just remember when you go into the courthouse, you're starting a new beginning.'

It was a quarter to eleven when Julia parked near the massive government building and climbed out of the white van she and Rhonda used for catering.

The day was already extremely warm and a stiff southerly breeze whipped the flags out in front of the courthouse and plastered Julia's cotton dress against her long legs as she made her way across the parking lot and into the building.

After seeking directions from a security guard, she eventually found herself several floors up and in the office of the judge's secretary, a middle-aged woman with hair the color of steel and red wire-rimmed glasses perched on the end of her nose.

"Did you have an appointment, Mrs. Warren?"

"Yes. I believe so. I'm with Southwestern Catering. We're to do a—"

"Oh, yes, of course," the woman said pleasantly, looking up and giving Julia a faint smile. "Why don't you have a seat? There's someone with Judge Hargrove at the moment, but I'm sure he won't be long."

Julia nodded. "Thank you," she said politely and crossed the room to take a seat on a short leather couch.

The secretary returned to her typing and the rapid tap-tap filled the quiet room. Julia glanced nervously around at the darkly paneled walls and thickly carpeted floors and wondered why, on today of all days, Rhonda's darn filling had chosen to fall out.

About five minutes later a tall blond man carrying a briefcase and wearing a harried expression came out of a door to Julia's right. He went straight out of the office, shutting the door none too quietly behind him.

Frowning at the door, the secretary reached for her intercom. "Judge, a Mrs. Warren is here about your mother's party. Shall I send her in?"

His mother, Julia thought with surprise. All along, she'd been thinking that Mrs. Hargrove was the man's wife.

"Yes, send her in, Edith."

The secretary nodded at Julia. "Please go right in."

Julia rose and walked stiffly toward the polished wooden door. Before she could let herself think anything negative she opened it and stepped inside.

"Mrs. Warren," a deep voice said from across the room, "won't you come in and have a seat?"

Chapter Two

Julia looked in the direction of the voice and her breath stopped somewhere in her throat. The man at the desk was far from what she'd expected. He was young. Far younger than what she thought a judge would, or even could, be. Of course, he might be older and merely look young for his age, but she doubted it. Judging by his appearance, he probably wasn't a day past thirty-five.

When Julia reached his desk, he stood and extended his hand. Julia reached out and his warm fingers touched hers briefly.

"Just call me Harry," he said, then arched a questioning brow at her. "And your name is?"

She didn't want to get on a first-name basis with this man. She was here for a job and nothing else. But she didn't want to appear unfriendly, either. "Julia," she murmured.

He nodded for her to take a cushioned seat directly in front of the desk, then eased back down into his own high-backed leather chair. "I hope it won't offend you if I eat a sandwich while we talk. I'm afraid things are running close today. If I don't eat now I won't have a chance until tonight."

Julia sat down and folded her hands nervously in her lap. She didn't want to lift her head and look at the man, but she forced herself to. "Please go ahead," she told him politely.

She couldn't prevent her gaze from gliding over his features. He was a dynamic-looking man. Dark hair was combed straight back from a broad forehead. His eyes were dark and deep-set, his nose slightly hawklike at the bridge as if he might have Indian blood in him. He was smiling at her, his lips pulled back to show a row of even white teeth.

"Would you like coffee, Julia?" he asked. "Of course you would," he went on before she had a chance to respond.

To Julia's amazement he rose to his feet and crossed the room. In one corner there was a small table holding a coffeemaker and cups. He proceeded to pour her one, glancing over his shoulder to ask, "Cream or sugar?"

Julia didn't want coffee. She wanted to be gone from here. But she could hardly get up and leave without a reasonable excuse. "Black will be fine," she said.

As he carried the coffee over to her, Julia found herself taking a further inventory of his appearance. He was a tall man, with a muscular physique his stylish clothes could not hide. Julia didn't know what judges wore under their robes, but she'd always figured it was dark, somber suits. This man had on light-gray pleated trousers, a red pin-striped shirt, gray dress suspenders and a gray-and-red patterned tie. He looked anything but somber.

"Thank you," she told him as she accepted the cup of coffee.

"It wasn't you I talked with this morning, was it? I think I remember her saying her name was Rhonda— Rhonda Genoa." He went back around the desk and took his seat.

"That was my partner," Julia told him, forcing her voice to be strong and steady. "She was unable to come this morning."

He shook his head and began to unwrap the foil from a sandwich. It was whole wheat bread and to Julia's amazement she could see peanut butter and jelly oozing from the edges.

The man was a judge, for Pete's sake! Julia figured he'd go out to a restaurant and have a full-course meal for lunch. Instead he was eating Christopher's favorite snack.

"It makes no difference really. I just happened to notice the different names." He took a bite of the sandwich, then pulled out a drawer to his right and began searching through the contents. "I made a list of sorts," he said, "but to be honest I haven't the foggiest idea what I'm doing."

Julia didn't know what she was doing, either. She'd come here expecting to feel a cool dislike for Judge Hargrove. Instead she was flushed and disconcerted and extremely aware of him as a man.

"It doesn't matter," she said. "Just so you have a general idea of what you'd like in the way of food and decorations. We'll take care of the rest."

He pulled out a small square of paper. "Here it is," he announced while reaching for a pair of black-framed glasses. Sliding them on and picking up a gold pen, he quickly scanned the list. "You see," he explained, "my younger sister usually does these things. But she married a few months ago and moved away. I've never organized a party in my life, but Mother would be disappointed if there weren't a few guests and a table of food to cheer her up.''

''Cheer her?'' Julia couldn't help asking. ''I thought this was a birthday party.''

Harris Hargrove laughed. The sound was low and very masculine. Julia found herself studying his face again and wondering at the man behind it.

''It is. But it's Mother's sixtieth. She'd rather be forty, or at the most fifty-nine.''

Reaching for his coffee cup, he looked across the desk at Julia. She could see now that his eyes were brown. They had a warm, faintly appraising look as they traveled over her face. ''A friend recommended your catering service. I believe your specialty is barbecue, isn't it?''

Julia nodded. ''Yes. Is that what you had in mind? Or would you like something more formal?''

He sipped his coffee as he continued to look at her. Julia wasn't sure if he was thinking about her or the party. Whichever, she found his gaze very disarming. Her heart was pounding and she felt sure her cheeks were pinker than the blush she'd applied earlier that morning.

''No. I don't want anything formal. I want it to be casual and relaxed.''

''Have you considered whether you want the party to be outside or inside?''

''Outside. By the pool, I think. Mother's an outdoor lady.'' He tapped his pen against the ink blotter on his desk. ''Barbecue would be appropriate for that, wouldn't it?''

''Of course. That is, if your mother likes barbecue. Since the party is in her honor, we shouldn't serve something she doesn't care for,'' Julia said.

"Oh, she likes it," he assured her. "Especially chicken. Me, I prefer ribs, but my taste doesn't count this time."

Julia decided her coffee had cooled enough to drink. She carefully took a sip and, as she did, glanced around the large room. It was darkly paneled like the outer office, but the windows that overlooked the street gave the room plenty of light. Oil paintings of early Oklahoma life hung here and there on the walls. Behind Harris Hargrove's desk were several plaques and certificates. She squinted her eyes in an effort to make out the small print on the one certifying his law degree. She noted with some surprise, as the words swam into focus, it was from Harvard.

Realizing he'd spoken to her, Julia jerked her gaze back to him. "I'm sorry. I didn't catch your question."

Harris smiled faintly at her and leaned back in his chair. Julia Warren, he thought, was a striking woman, tall and curved in all the right places. As for her age, she looked about twenty-five. Her ivory skin was as smooth as milk. And those eyes and lips... Suddenly he felt a little ashamed of himself for admiring a married woman. But it would be hard for any man not to notice her light gray eyes. They had a haunting, seductive quality that pulled at him.

"I was asking if you also made desserts," he said, his eyes going discreetly to her left hand. There was a narrow band on her ring finger, but maybe it was there for other reasons. Maybe she was divorced, he considered hopefully, and hadn't yet quit wearing the ring or dropped the Mrs. God only knew how many divorces he saw pass through the courts. Still, it was difficult to imagine any man letting this woman slip away.

Julia nodded. "Yes, we do serve desserts. Traditional birthday cakes or several other things. Some plain, some fancy. We try to cater to all tastes."

Sitting forward in the chair, he took another bite of his sandwich. After he chewed and swallowed he asked, "Have you been in business long?"

Julia didn't think his question was relevant, but she answered just the same. "Three years. It started out with only barbecue, but when my friend began to work with me, we decided to expand a bit."

"I see. Well, to start off with, I think I'll keep it small. Say, a hundred guests. And the barbecue sounds good."

So he considered a hundred guests a small party, she thought wryly. "If you'd like we can have it assorted. Chicken, and perhaps brisket and ribs. Do you want a sit-down dinner, or a buffet, eat-when-you-like thing?"

"The latter, I think. To keep it casual."

Julia set her coffee on the edge of the desk and reached for her purse. "I'd better make notes to keep this all straight," she told him, pulling out a pad and pencil.

Harris watched her rich auburn hair fall forward as she bent over the notepad. It was well past her shoulders and the thick, natural curl gave her a bohemian look. Long, black beaded earrings dangled from her ears, matching her black-and-white summer dress.

She wore little makeup but with her natural beauty she didn't need it. In fact, Mrs. Julia Warren was one of the most beautiful women he'd seen in a long time.

He cleared his throat, hoping it would also clear his thoughts. It wasn't like him to take such notice of a woman. Women were a luxury he didn't allow himself. Not in his line of work. "As far as the rest of the meal goes," he went on, "I'll leave that up to you."

"The dessert?" she asked without looking up.

Damn, he wished she wasn't married, he thought in spite of himself. "A big white cake. You know, the kind with roses and candles and all that sort of thing. I think Mother would like that."

Julia noticed the way his voice held a different inflection when he spoke of Mrs. Hargrove. The warm fondness that only genuine love could produce. It surprised her. Not because he loved his mother. But because he so obviously showed it.

"Ice cream?"

He didn't answer right away and she glanced up to see he was busy chewing another bite of gooey sandwich. Nodding, he swallowed and said, "Vanilla. Some things are better when they're not dressed up, don't you think?"

Julia, for some unexplained reason, was suddenly wondering if he was talking about his food or his women. Or did he have women in his life? she wondered. Damn it, Julia, she quickly scolded herself, since when have you wondered about a man's love life?

"I think vanilla is the perfect choice," she agreed without meeting his gaze. "Now we get down to decorations. Is there a certain theme you'd like for the party?"

"As I told you before, I don't know anything about parties. I rarely attend them. So you do whatever you think best. Maybe some flowers here and there, nothing elaborate."

The intercom on his desk buzzed. Harris leaned over and pressed a button. Julia couldn't help but notice the way his shoulders flexed beneath the fine fabric of his shirt. "Yes, Edith?"

"Sorry to disturb you, Judge. There's a Mr. Lawson here from the firm of Lawson, Daly, Lawson. He says he's the defending attorney for the bribery case you'll be hearing next week."

Harris frowned as he digested the secretary's reply. "Mr. Lawson has no business with me."

There was a long pause, then the secretary came back with, "He's very adamant, Judge."

Julia thought he muttered an oath under his breath. "Tell Mr. Lawson there will be no more continuances, no more delays."

"I, er, think you just told him, Judge."

Apparently satisfied he'd made himself clear, Harris leaned back in his chair, his gaze on Julia once again. "Sorry about the interruption."

Julia found her eyes drawn to his and her heart jolted as he smiled at her in an easy, familiar way. It was such a contradiction to the unyielding man of only a moment ago.

"I'm taking up more of your time than I should," she said, starting to rise.

"No. Please sit," he said firmly. "I have fifteen more minutes before I have to be in court."

She wondered what sort of case he'd be hearing and then wondered why it should matter to her.

As though reading her thoughts, Harris said, "It's a child-abuse case and I'm not looking forward to presiding over it."

He removed his glasses and in a weary gesture pinched the bridge of his nose. For a moment Julia's heart almost softened toward him. Then he went on, "But you're not here to listen to my problems. You're here about a party." He smiled again. "Can you think of anything else you need to know?"

Julia took a deep breath as she scanned the few notes she'd scribbled on her pad. "Uh, well, what about dishes, cutlery? Do you want to provide them? Or would you prefer us to?"

He shrugged, then gave a low chuckle. "I don't know. You tell me. Can't we use paper plates? The kind you can throw away and forget about?"

Her lips twitched with amusement as she began to write again. He certainly wasn't worried about making a big impression. "Well, that is casual."

"And uncouth?" he asked catching the hesitation in her voice, then waved his own question away as she glanced up at him. "But I'll let you decide. I don't think it'd bother Mother one way or the other. The food and the guests will be the most important thing with her."

Julia tended to agree with him. People were what made a party, but she could hardly go around voicing that opinion when she was in the catering business. "We'll find something suitable, Mr. Hargrove," she told him. "However, there is another thing to consider. Do you have an alternate plan in case the weather is bad?"

"Not really. There's a large game room in the house that connects to the living room. And we could put the buffet in the dining room. Would that work?"

"If necessary we'll make it work," she told him, then closed her notepad and gave him a stiff smile. "Well, I guess that's all I need. If you think of anything else you'd like for us to prepare please give us a call."

"Are you sure you don't need to know anything else?" he asked, wishing he could have more time with her. He didn't really know why, except that she was like a breath of fresh air. And fresh air before a trial was like a dose of much-needed vitamins.

Nodding, Julia rose to her feet. "Thank you, Mr. Hargrove, for allowing us to do this party for you. I assure you we'll do our best to make it a success." She struggled to remain cool and professional as she extended her hand to him.

Smiling, he got to his feet and took her offered hand. "Please. Call me Harry, and it's been a pleasure, Julia. I'm sure you'll do a fine job. And if you have any questions at all just give me a call. I'll do my best to get back to you."

He slowly let go of her hand and Julia edged around the chair and started toward the door. The foolish pounding of her heart made her want to run as fast and hard as she could, and the feeling intensified as he followed closely behind her.

At the door he reached around her and gave the knob a quick flick. She glanced up at him as the door swung open and found herself almost wanting to bask in the warm, appreciative look in his eyes.

"Goodbye, Julia. See you at the party."

Not if she could help it, Julia thought desperately. "Goodbye, Mr. Hargrove, er, Harris, and thank you again."

Before anything else could be said, Julia hurried out of the room and passed through the secretary's office. By the time she got out of the building and to the van, she'd gathered most of her senses. Yet she was angrier with herself than she'd ever been.

She'd actually said "thank-you" to a judge! What in the world had gotten into her? All the time she'd been in his office she'd been unable to quit looking at him. At his features, his clothes, his body. She'd watched his every expression, listened to his deep voice and wondered about the kind of person he was. She couldn't believe she'd let herself think of him as a man. He was the enemy. Someone just like him had set the killer free who'd taken Carl's life. How could she have forgotten that? Even for a minute?

Chapter Three

"Mommy, can I go with you and Auntie Rhonda tonight?"

Julia turned to look at her son, who was perched on a work counter, a clump of modeling clay between his legs, which he was working with his small but determined hands. "I think so. If you promise to stay in the kitchen and be very good and quiet."

He pursed his little lips. "You say that every time. And I'm good every time."

Julia hid her smile as she turned back to the job of chopping green onions. "You weren't good this morning when you opened Josephine's cage."

Christopher wagged his head back and forth. "She didn't hurt nothin'."

"No, but she could have," Julia gently admonished. "Josephine doesn't know the things that can hurt her. Just like Tommy's baby brother, Louis."

"He can't play in the yard," Christopher said.

"No, he isn't big enough yet. But he will be soon," she said. One of her neighbors had a new baby son, and Christopher was fascinated by him.

Chris carefully set the tiny man he'd made on the counter, then pinched off another piece of clay. "Mommy?"

"Hmm?" she asked absently as she raked the onions into a bowl of crumbled cornbread.

"Can I have a baby brother? Like Louis?"

Christopher had asked this question before and Julia still didn't know exactly how to answer it.

"Well, what do you say, Mommy?" Rhonda asked from behind her. Julia turned to see her friend coming into the work room, her arms laden with two sacks of groceries. "Sounds like a worthwhile project to me," Rhonda added as she placed the sacks on an empty table.

"It's not that simple," Julia told her son while arching a menacing brow at Rhonda. "There has to be a daddy to have a baby brother or sister, and we don't have a daddy."

"Maybe you could find one," Chris said innocently. "Maybe there's a daddy somewhere who'd like me and Josephine."

Rhonda walked up and ruffled Christopher's hair. "There is, honey. And he's just waiting for your mommy to find him."

"Rhonda!" Julia scolded. "Don't push it!"

Rhonda merely laughed as she tied a white apron over her slacks and blouse.

Julia reached for a stalk of celery. "Get the tooth fixed?"

"Yes. After waiting two hours in the dentist's office."

"How does it feel now?"

"Ask me later when the numbness wears off."

Carefully cradling the little man he'd made of clay, Chris climbed down from the work counter. "Can I take my soldiers out in the yard and play in the sandpile?" he asked his mother.

Julia looked down at him, relieved that he'd forgotten about a baby brother. At least for the moment. "Of course you may. Just don't go out the gate and into Rhonda's yard."

"I won't," he promised, his stocky little legs already racing for the door.

"So," Rhonda mused aloud, after the child had left the room, "Chris is asking for a brother."

"It's nothing new," Julia said with a shrug. "He's asked before."

"What do you tell him?" Rhonda began putting the groceries away, but she glanced on and off at Julia.

"I just try to explain that we aren't like other families." She turned a helpless expression on her friend. "But it makes me feel guilty, Rhonda. I know Chris is missing out. There're so many things I can't give him now that Carl is dead."

Rhonda gave her a sympathetic smile. "You shouldn't feel guilty about anything. You didn't ask to be a widow."

"No. But I am just the same." Julia turned back to the salad she was preparing and began to chop the stalks of celery.

"It won't always be like this, Julia," Rhonda continued.

"What does that mean?" Julia asked wearily. The celery chopped, she scooped it off the cutting board and tossed it in with the other ingredients.

"You're young. You'll find a man for you and Chris."

Grimacing, Julia looked over her shoulder at her friend. "I'm not going out hunting for a man just because Chris wants a brother or sister."

Rhonda's brows rose. "I didn't say you should. I think you need a companion, not stud services."

Julia snorted as she headed toward the refrigerator. "I don't think I need either one. Besides, I don't see you looking." She pulled a pitcher of tea from the shelf, then filled a glass with ice.

Rhonda laughed and reached up to fluff her short black hair. "No. But I'm going to start. Bobby Genoa is a forgotten man. In fact, I agreed to go out with my cousin's friend on Monday night. You remember the one I met at Christmas? He called this morning to tell me he has tickets to a little-theater production of *Oklahoma!*"

"Oh? This is news. Isn't he the businessman you labeled stuffy?"

Rhonda smiled hesitantly. "I did. But since then I've decided a businessman might be just what I need. Bobby was a macho man and he ended up not being my type at all."

"I can't argue with that," Julia agreed, remembering how Rhonda and Bobby had fought continually right up until their divorce. She didn't want to see that happen to Rhonda again. "Just be careful."

"Are you kidding? I'm thinking about having a questionnaire printed up and passing them out to potential dates. 'Careful' is going to be my middle name." She glanced at Julia. "Did you stop by the market for strawberries?"

"I did. I also picked up a few more things I thought would stay fresh for next week." Julia sat down at the table and took a long drink of iced tea. She'd been working steadily since her meeting with Harris Hargrove. She'd gotten a lot done in preparation for tonight's dinner. But she hadn't made much progress with getting the man out of her mind.

Rhonda looked up at the wall clock over the sink. "Two hours until the Gilmores are expecting us. I suppose I'll go ahead with the dinner rolls." She crossed the room to where another row of cabinets stretched across the wall and began to bring down flour, salt and other ingredients.

It was hard to believe that this spacious kitchen had once been a garage where Carl had tinkered with cars—his own and his friends. Shortly after Julia had decided to go into the catering business, she'd hired carpenters to come in and change the building into a place where she could work and store everything necessary for the business.

Now there were rows of shiny white metal cabinets lining three walls, a restaurant-size stove top with eight gas burners, two freezers and a huge refrigerator. Three large ovens, one of them at eye level, made sure they were never caught without enough baking space. A deep, double stainless-steel sink and dishwasher sat below a window that overlooked Julia's backyard. It had taken more money than Julia cared to think about to go into the catering business. But now it was paying off. Far more than she'd ever expected.

"How did the meeting with the judge go?" Rhonda asked.

Julia purposely took another swallow of her tea before she answered. "So-so."

The evasive answer made Rhonda cast her friend an impatient look. "Well, did you get all the information we needed?"

Julia answered cautiously, not wanting to let Rhonda know just how much Judge Hargrove had disturbed her.

"I think so. I took down a few notes. It's to be outside, a hundred guests, assorted barbecue for the main course. Cake and ice cream for dessert."

Rhonda nodded. "What about decorations?"

"Simple. He's leaving that up to us. Along with the dishes. He said we could use paper, but I really hate to."

"Why? Because of who the Hargroves are, or because of the heavy food?"

"Both, I suppose. I hate for things to look chintzy. I think we should take the earthenware."

"Whatever you say is all right with me," Rhonda told her, then asked, "What about the time? I hope it's not going to be any earlier than seven, or it's going to be hotter than a firecracker."

The question had Julia frantically searching her mind. "I . . . uh, we didn't discuss a time."

Rhonda stared at her in disbelief. "Didn't discuss a time," she parroted. "You are kidding, aren't you?"

Julia's face reddened with embarrassment. She'd dealt with dozens of clients since she'd been in the catering business and not once had she forgotten to ask such a vital question. "No, I'm afraid I'm not. Time never came up in our conversation."

"Well, surely you confirmed the day?"

Julia's head swung back and forth. "The day didn't come up in our conversation, either."

Rhonda looked stunned. "Good Lord, Julia, you didn't make a fool of yourself right in the middle of things, did you?"

That all depended on how one wanted to look at it, Julia thought wryly. "I didn't start mouthing off about my low opinion of the judical system, if that's what you mean."

Rhonda let out a long sigh of relief. "Thank goodness. It would certainly never do to make enemies of the Hargroves. Not when they can send lots of business our way." She turned back to the counter and began sifting cups of flour into a large mixing bowl.

"Still," she said through a cloud of white powder. "I can't imagine you forgetting to ask about the time or date."

Julia swallowed, surprised that the memory of Judge Hargrove was almost as distracting as being in his presence. "I was nervous," she said quickly. "Anyway, you know how I felt about all this."

"So. What was the man like? Bald and sixtyish? I only talked with his secretary over the phone. She left me with the impression that Mrs. Hargrove was an older woman."

"She is. Sixty, to be exact," Julia said. "And she's not his wife. She's his mother."

Rhonda's expression was speculative as she turned to face Julia. "And how old is Judge Hargrove?"

Julia's eyes skittered away from her friend's. "I'd say thirty-four, thirty-five."

"Then he probably wasn't bald, either," Rhonda concluded with a gleam in her eye.

"Actually he had a thick head of dark hair," Julia said without thinking.

"Hmm, tell me more," Rhonda insisted as she dusted flour from her hands.

Frowning, Julia rose to her feet. "You have dinner rolls to make. And I have quail to attend to."

"Uh-uh. We've got a few minutes to spare and I want to hear about this judge. I knew something was fishy. You've never been so neglectful about important details."

Julia hurried over to one of the tall upright freezers. "I told you. I was nervous. The man's a judge. Although I will say he didn't look or behave as you might expect a judge to."

"Really? How do you mean?"

Julia shrugged and opened the door. Freezing white vapor rushed out at her. "I don't know. I just mean he doesn't fit the stereotype."

Rhonda thoughtfully tapped her finger against her chin. "I don't know what the stereotype of a judge is."

Julia knew her friend was goading her. "I expected him to be full of himself. Superior acting."

"And he wasn't?"

Julia slowly sorted through the packages on the wire rack. "Well, he was eating a peanut-butter-and-jelly sandwich for lunch. And he fetched me a cup of coffee himself. You'd have thought he'd have ordered his secretary to do that."

"You had coffee with the man?" Rhonda suddenly grinned. "Was he good-looking?"

"Now what makes you ask that?" Finding what she was looking for, Julia pulled two packages from the shelves and carried her load to a wide butcher block.

"I'm habitually nosy, so tell me."

"I don't know what you consider good-looking."

"Oh, come off it, and quit stalling," Rhonda scolded.

Knowing that Rhonda wouldn't hush until her curiosity was satisfied, Julia said, "He was more striking-looking than what you'd call handsome. He was a big man, dressed fashionably, and for the most part, very congenial." Almost too congenial, Julia decided. She began to unwrap the freezer paper from a quail breast. As she worked, a tiny frown creased her forehead. "But I just wonder what kind of judge he really is. My guess would be very lenient." She practically snarled the last word, making Rhonda roll her eyes with impatience.

"I suppose you could tell that just by discussing a birthday party," Rhonda drawled.

"Well, aren't they all?" Julia retorted.

"Look Julia, not all people who wind up in court are guilty. If you or I were the accused, you'd be praying for a little leniency from a judge."

Julia's lips tightened to a thin line. She didn't want to consider Rhonda's reasoning. For four years she'd blamed a judge and the system for Carl's death. It was impossible to suddenly put those feelings aside. Still, she wondered if Harris Hargrove was a compassionate man.

"I hope I'm never in that situation." She couldn't imagine having her future in the hands of Harris Hargrove.

Wrinkling her nose at Julia, Rhonda went back to making the rolls, and for the next few minutes both women were steeped in their own thoughts.

It was Rhonda who eventually spoke again. "You'll have to get back in touch with him, you know."

"What?" Julia asked absently as she glanced out the window to make sure Christopher was still where he should be.

"The judge," Rhonda said with a note of impatience. "You'll have to contact him again to get the time and day of the party. I believe his secretary said next Saturday, but we can hardly guess about something so important."

Julia opened her mouth to voice a loud no, then quickly decided against it. She didn't want to make an issue over this thing. Not when Rhonda was already viewing Julia's behavior as strange. She'd call his secretary and get the needed information. "Yes, I will. No problem," Julia said blithely.

But to herself Julia prayed the party would be soon so that the whole thing would be over with. The less she had to deal with Harris Hargrove, the better.

The Gilmore dinner went off without a hitch. In fact, Mr. Gilmore was so pleased he included a hefty tip with his payment for their services.

The next day Rhonda took her half of the extra profit and went shopping with her mother. Julia tucked hers away in a jar she'd labeled ''vacation.'' Since Christopher had been only a few weeks old when Carl had been killed, the past four years had been difficult in more ways than one for Julia. Carl's salary as a policeman had not been that substantial, making it nearly impossible for them to save. The insurance premium she'd received after his death had been poured into the catering business. She and Chris had lived meagerly for the first two years. But this past year business had doubled and things were looking brighter. She'd promised Chris and herself a real vacation by the ocean. Something her son had never seen.

''Can we go to the park today, Mommy? And get ice cream?''

Julia guided the vacuum cleaner around her son as she pushed it over the bedroom carpet. ''Maybe. Have you fed Josephine and given her fresh water?''

''Yes. And she pecked my finger.''

''She's a naughty bird.''

''She is not naughty,'' Chris instantly defended his feathered pet. ''She wants out so she can hop around. Like this.'' He proceeded to imitate the bird, jumping around the room and giving a few screeches and squawks.

''She probably would like to hop around,'' Julia agreed, ''but she's going to stay exactly where she is.''

Christopher carefully timed himself and jumped over the vacuum just as his mother pushed it by him.

"Christopher! Be careful!"

He laughed with typical little-boy mischief and hopped up onto the carefully made bed. Julia clicked the upright off and gave her son a pointed look. "Your jeans are dirty and now you're sitting on my white bedspread. What am I going to do with you?"

Christopher giggled. "Take me to the park."

"I think I'll tickle you silly instead," Julia said, crouching over, then pouncing at the child.

Shrieks of laughter filled the room as Christopher attempted to evade his mother's clutches. Julia grabbed him around the waist and proceeded to tickle him up and down his ribs.

"Now are you going to be a good boy?" Julia chuckled as she flopped him onto his back.

The child's freckled face was red with exertion and his laughter had turned into helpless hiccups. "I'll be good, Mommy," he promised.

Julia leaned down and pressed a kiss on his forehead, then smothered both his cheeks with kisses, laughing all the while. Christopher began to howl in protest. Amidst all the mayhem the telephone rang.

Julia released her son and quickly skirted around the bed, shushing the child with a finger pressed to her lips as she reached for the phone on the night table.

"Hello," she answered cheerfully.

"Is this Mrs. Julia Warren?"

The male voice was vaguely familiar and Julia struggled to identify the caller. "Yes. It is."

"This is Harris Hargrove. You came to my office yesterday."

Julia was instantly alert. "Yes. Of course. I'm glad you called. In fact, I was getting ready to call you."

"Really?"

"Yes, I—I'm afraid we neglected to discuss the time and day of the party."

"Oh. I see."

He sounded disappointed. For the life of her, Julia couldn't imagine why. "Is there a problem?" she asked quickly. "You weren't calling to cancel the party, were you?"

"Oh, no. Not at all. I only wanted to make sure you had all the information you needed."

Actually, after Julia had left his office yesterday, Harris had made a few quick calls and discovered Julia Warren was a widow. Now he was trying to think of an excuse to see her again. "And I thought perhaps you'd like to see the place where you'll be setting up the party."

"I wouldn't want to bother you today," she answered quickly. "My partner and I can come early on the day of the party and look everything over."

Harris frowned with annoyance when he noticed the light flashing on his telephone, indicating a caller was waiting. "It would help you to see the layout of things, wouldn't it?" he persisted.

"Yes, but like I said—"

"It's really no bother, Julia. I have the afternoon off. I'd be happy to show you around."

He said her name as if he'd known her for years. Julia took an anxious breath. "To be honest, I've promised to take my son to the park, and since I rarely get an afternoon off myself, I'd hate to disappoint him."

Rhonda was going to kill her for this, Julia thought. But something told her that Harris Hargrove's call had nothing to do with the upcoming party, and she didn't know how to deal with that notion, or with him.

So she had a child, Harris was thinking. Yesterday, when he talked to a friend who'd used Southwestern Catering and discovered Julia was a widow, he'd felt compassion for her. Now that he knew she'd been raising a child alone, he had to add admiration to his feelings.

"Bring him with you," he quickly told her. "The grounds around the house are large and fenced in. He can explore to his heart's content. Even go for a swim in the pool."

Julia hesitated, her mind spinning. What was this man up to?

"Julia, can he swim?"

She realized her thoughts had wandered. "Er, yes. Very well, actually. He's been taking lessons this summer at the Y, but I don't think—"

Christopher, who overheard his mother discussing swimming, scooted off the bed and tugged on the leg of her jeans.

"Yes, Mommy. I want to swim! Yeah! Yeah!"

Harris could hear the child's excited voice in the background and smiled to himself. "How can you say no to that?"

Julia passed a hand over her forehead. The judge was a client, she told herself, and she might seem negligent if she refused to look over the party spot. Besides, with Christopher with her, what could possibly happen?

"I suppose I can't," she answered a bit wearily.

"Great! Why don't you come over about twelve. You know the address, don't you? Cook will have something prepared for lunch."

Julia started to protest. "I don't think lunch—"

"I won't eat until you get here," he said, not giving her the opportunity to argue. "See you then, Julia."

The phone clicked in her ear. It was a moment or two before Julia realized she might as well put the receiver back on its hook. As she did she stared thoughtfully into space. The man had maneuvered her. But why?

"Mommy, are we going swimming? Where? Where?"

Julia glanced idly down at her son. "Across town. At a client's."

"What's a cli-client?" he asked curiously.

This particular client was more than she'd bargained for, she thought. "It's a person who hires us to cook for them," she hastily explained, then glanced at her watch. It was a quarter to eleven. And it would take at least thirty minutes to get to Judge Hargrove's place. "Hurry to your room, Chris. We have to change clothes before we can go."

"Yippee! I'm going swimming," he squealed, turning on his toe to take off in a run across the hall to his room.

Sighing, Julia began to wind the electrical cord back around the upright. The last thing she wanted was to see Judge Harris Hargrove. She'd spent the better part of the previous night trying to push the man's image from her mind, and the effort had left her feeling down and somewhat guilty.

Carl's memory had always been the one she'd carried with her into her dreams. She'd never wanted or allowed another man to take that place. But the judge's image had persistently invaded her mind in spite of her efforts to push it out.

With a shake of her head, she shoved the vacuum into the closet. It would do no good to try to analyze her reaction to Harris Hargrove. Besides, the man was merely hiring her services, and he wanted to make sure the party went smoothly. That's all there was to his invitation.

Julia kept reminding herself of that as she helped Christopher change his clothes.

"Is Auntie Rhonda going to go with us?" Christopher asked as Julia adjusted the waistband of his neon-printed shorts.

"No. She's gone shopping with her mother today." Julia could just imagine the look on Rhonda's face when she found out about this lunch meeting with the judge. She would instantly read all sorts of things into it. Julia picked up her son's tennis shoes and quickly tied them on his feet. "You're all ready, so go into the living room and talk with Josephine while I finish getting ready, okay? But no feeding her crackers."

Christopher nodded as he trotted out of the room. Julia crossed the hall and went straight to her bedroom closet. After a quick glance through her clothes, she picked out a pair of white slacks and a nautical-style blouse in white and navy blue.

She told herself that she wouldn't take pains to look nice for the judge. But she did take time to apply a touch of makeup and tie her unruly red hair back with a white scarf, telling herself it would make a bad impression on the business if she looked unkempt.

Chapter Four

Christopher chattered nonstop as Julia drove the two of them through the quiet well-to-do neighborhood where Harris Hargrove lived. Julia patiently answered his questions while keeping her eye out for the correct house number.

She rarely traveled through this part of the city. The few times she had were the occasions she'd been catering a party. Julia couldn't imagine living on a big estate with a beautiful, carefully manicured lawn such as she was passing now.

She had come from a farm family, who'd been short on money but long on love. And when she'd married Carl at the age of nineteen, she hadn't expected him to make her rich on a policeman's salary. Julia supposed having wealth was nice, but she had always been one who believed wealth was really a state of the heart.

"Here it is, Chris," she said as she pulled up in front of number 3002. "Now promise me you'll be a gentleman."

"I promise," he said, with great dignity, but Julia could tell he was itching to bounce excitedly on the seat.

She turned the van into the paved driveway, which was long and curving, and deeply shaded by towering oaks and maples. As they drew nearer, Julia noticed the house was a huge L-shaped structure made of brick that at one time she suspected had been red but was now weathered to a rosy pink. On the east section of the building, beginning a few feet from the portico, thick green ivy clung tenaciously to the wall, covering it completely. Julia thought the effect was rather English and wondered if there was a rose garden in the back. If there was, though, she doubted the judge tended it. He hardly seemed the gardening type.

"Wow!" Christopher exclaimed as Julia pulled the van to a halt in the drive circling in front of the house. "This is bigger than the park. And look, Mommy!" He pointed back in the direction they'd just come. Two squirrels were scampering around an ornamental birdbath.

"Yes, the squirrels are getting a drink." She reached over and unlatched Chris's seat belt, then brushed his tawny hair to one side of his forehead.

"Hello. I see you made it."

Julia turned at the sound of a man's voice. Judge Hargrove was walking toward them, dressed in khaki trousers and a tan-and-white patterned sports shirt. His appearance was just as compelling as it had been yesterday.

"Yes," she said out the open window. "It was no problem to find."

He moved to open the door for her. Julia climbed out, then reached back inside for Christopher. When the child was out and standing quietly beside his mother, Harris leaned down and shook his hand.

"What's your name, young man?"

Christopher glanced first at his mother for reassurance, then up at the tall, dark man. "Christopher C. Warren," he said proudly.

"Well, hello, Christopher. My name is Harry. Are you and your mother ready for lunch?"

Christopher nodded. "I'm real hungry. Mommy wouldn't let me eat before we came."

Harris smiled down at the boy. "Mother's are like that sometimes. But I'll bet Cook has made some stuff you'll like. How about brownies?"

"Yeah!" Christpher exclaimed, his blue eyes alight.

"What about you, Mother?" he asked, slanting Julia an amused glance.

She nodded, not really knowing how to take his familiar attitude. This was supposed to be a business meeting, but she feared she'd been right to suspect he would treat it as something else. The whole idea left her feeling very unsettled.

"Good," he said, taking her elbow and guiding her toward the entrance of the house. "I believe lunch is waiting, so let's go right on in."

Christopher skipped ahead of them until he reached the double wooden doors, then turned and looked up at the judge. "Is this your house, Harry?"

"It sure is. What do you think of it so far?"

"It's big," he said with typical childlike candor.

Harris chuckled. "That's what the housekeeper says, too."

They stepped into a small foyer that felt blessedly cool compared to the afternoon heat. Julia kept Christopher's hand firmly ensconced in hers as Harris led them down a step and into a long room that, like the exterior of the house, had a certain English flavor.

She'd barely had time to glance at the chintz curtains on the windows when they turned through an open door and walked down a short hall.

"The dining room is this way," Harris said. "Would you like to wash up first?"

Julia glanced down at her son. "I think Chris managed to keep his hands clean on the drive over."

"She probably made you wash just before you got into the car, didn't she?" he asked the boy.

Wide-eyed, Christopher asked, "How did you know?"

Harris gave him an impish wink. "Because I was your size once, and I was notorious for getting dirty."

Julia watched a look of awe spread across her son's face as he stared up at the tall man. "You were like me once?"

Harris nodded, then added with a low chuckle, "Only I probably wasn't nearly as polite. My mother called me Horrible Harry."

This made the child laugh and Julia felt her own lips tilting upward at the thought of Judge Hargrove as a rambunctious youngster.

The three of them entered the dining room. To Julia's relief it wasn't nearly as formal as she'd feared. It, too, had English overtones, right down to the oak sideboard standing against one wall and the silver tea set gracing the long dining table.

Harris found a thick telephone book to put on Christopher's chair, then Julia lifted her son onto it. She turned to find Harris waiting to help her into her own high-backed chair.

She murmured a thank-you, and for a few seconds he lingered at her shoulder, his expression warm as he looked down at her.

Uncomfortable with his nearness, Julia quickly turned her attention to the table, discreetly clearing her throat as she did. Harris moved to the head of the table, just to Julia's right, and took a seat.

Instead of looking at him, Julia surveyed the food before her. There was a silver tray stacked with sandwiches, a bowl of fresh tossed salad and a soup tureen, which looked to be a beautiful antique piece of china, decorated with tiny rosebuds and gold-edged lacing.

Harris lifted its lid and sniffed. "Looks like Cook fixed alphabet," he told Christopher. "Do you like alphabet soup?"

Christopher nodded as he kept his hands obediently together in his lap. "Yes. But Mommy gets alphabet soup from a can."

Harris laughed and Julia smiled.

"I suspect that Cook did, too. He just put it in this bowl to make us think he worked hard." Harris ladled a small bowl full of the soup and passed it to Julia.

She placed it and a few crackers in front of her son, then helped him with his napkin and spoon.

Harris watched the two of them. So many battered and orphaned children came before him in court. It was good for the heart to see a child so obviously loved, even if he had only one parent.

"Soup for you, Julia?" Harris asked.

"No, I think I'll just have salad," she told him.

He handed her a plate and she busied herself piling it with crisp vegetables. Yet all the while her senses were consumed with his nearness.

He was a big man, and his undeniable presence reached out to her. From the corner of her eye she could see his hand. The tanned skin, the back sprinkled with black hair. The fingers were long and slightly squared at the tips, and there was a class ring on his fourth finger. Julia decided it was probably from Harvard where he'd earned his law degree.

"Since we talked this morning," he said as he filled his own plate with salad and sandwiches, "I've been thinking about the time for the party. I don't want the guests to wait around starving, but I believe any time before seven-thirty will simply be too hot."

"I agree," Julia said. "Seven thirty sounds good." She reached for the pepper shaker and sprinkled the seasoning liberally over her salad, then glanced up at him. He smiled at her. It was an expression that crinkled the corners of his dark eyes and dimpled one cheek. Julia tried hard not to be disarmed by it.

"I wish most of the lawyers I deal with were as easy to get along with as you are, Julia," he said.

Julia felt like an imposter. If he really knew what she thought about the legal system, he'd probably throw her out and cancel the whole deal. Yet to be honest with herself, she wasn't exactly sure what her opinion was of Harris Hargrove. Yet.

"It is your party, Mr. Hargrove," she said.

"Harry," he reminded her. "All my friends call me Harry."

He shifted his gaze back to his plate, but he knew without looking that she felt uncomfortable. He'd known that yesterday from the moment she'd walked into his office. Throughout his years in law, he's seen all sorts of people and judged all sorts of characters. He'd be willing to bet that Julia Warren wasn't normally a nervous person, yet she seemed very much on guard with him. And that intrigued him.

"I've also looked over my schedule for next week. I think the only safe date for me will be Sunday. Will that pose a problem for you?" he asked.

Julia shook her head as she stabbed a piece of lettuce with her fork. "I'm sure it will be fine," she told him. Normally she and Rhonda didn't work on Sundays unless it was something big. But Rhonda viewed the Hargrove party as something big.

"Actually," he went on, "Mother's birthday is Friday, but I know I'll be hung up in court that day unless the case has some unforeseen delay. But you can hardly prepare pounds of food on short notice," he reasoned, as he reached for the tray holding two pots and cups. "Would you like coffee or tea?" he asked.

"Either will be fine," she told him.

He proceeded to pour out two cups of tea and passed her one. "Milk and sugar?"

"Just a little sugar, please."

He passed her the bowl, saying, "There's nothing like a good cup of Earl Grey when you have the time to relax and enjoy it."

The cup was wafer-thin china and looked extremely fragile in his large hand. "I've never seen a man who prefers tea," she said, then felt self-conscious heat stain her cheeks. "I mean in this part of the country men are coffee drinkers."

His expression was amused rather than affronted. "You're right, and I do like coffee, too. But my mother is English and she taught me to appreciate a good cup of tea."

So that explained the house and its furnishing, Julia thought. In spite of herself she was curious. "How did your mother come to be in Oklahoma?"

Cup in hand, he leaned back against his chair, his eyes warm as he watched her little boy crumble crackers into his soup. Julia saw the tenderness in his expression and was surprised by it. She hadn't expected him to be so indulgent with her son.

Harris shifted his gaze to Julia's face. "Mother was born in London, but during the war her family moved to Brighton to get away from the bombing. My father was an American soldier stationed near Brighton. He met my mother there when she was only fifteen. They struck up a sort of friendship, but then he was sent to France and she thought she'd never see him again. Years later he was back in England on business and by chance, or fate, or whatever you want to call it, he ran into her. By then she'd grown into a beautiful woman. Dad fell in love immediately and Mother said she didn't have a chance once Dad started pursuing her. Romantic, don't you think?"

A hesitant smile touched Julia's lips. She'd never talked about romance with a man. Not even Carl. He'd been kind and responsible but he'd never been a romantic sort. She wondered if Harris was. "Yes, it does sound romantic. Lucky your mother's family was able to get out of London." She paused. "Do you still have relatives in London?" she asked.

"Yes, grandparents. My other set of grandparents live in Claremore. My grandfather just retired from the Bureau of Indian Affairs a couple of years ago."

"He's Indian?" Julia asked.

"Both of them are half Cherokee." A wry grin touched his mouth. "I'm a strange mix."

Julia didn't know about strange, but she knew he was very different from any man she'd been around. Of course, that wasn't saying much since she hadn't dated once since Carl's death.

"Can I have dessert now?" Christopher asked.

Julia looked at her son and saw he'd already finished eating his soup. "What about half a sandwich?" she suggested.

Christopher wrinkled his nose, then relented. "If I eat it, then can I have a brownie?"

"Yes, you may." As Julia handed him an egg-salad sandwich, she was very much aware of Harris's eyes on the two of them.

"Then can I go swimming?" Christopher wanted to know.

"In a little while, when Mommy can watch you."

Christopher wriggled impatiently on his chair, but didn't whine.

"I have a friend in the backyard you might like, Chris," Harris told the boy. "His name is Oscar."

Christopher's expression became eager. "Do you have a little boy like me?"

Smiling gently, Harris shook his head. "No, I'm not that lucky. But I have a dog. And he loves little boys."

Christopher's eyes grew wide with excitement. "A dog! Mommy, a dog!"

"We'll go see him as soon as we're finished with lunch," Harris promised.

Julia sipped her tea while wondering if she should thank Harris for being so kind to Christopher, or to be angry with him for making her visit a social one instead of a practical one.

Setting the cup back in its saucer, she looked over at him, determined to get things back to business. "So, does your mother know about the party? Or is it a surprise?"

Harris smiled fondly. "She doesn't know. And she's probably expecting me to work right through her birthday and forget all about it."

"Then she doesn't live here with you?" The house was certainly big enough for several people, Julia thought.

"This house was my mother and father's. But after he died, Mother found it too difficult to live here and deal with all the memories staring her in the face. She has a place of her own about twenty minutes from here."

Julia knew exactly how his mother must have felt. Sometimes she thought she was crazy for not selling the home she and Carl had shared. In fact, her parents had virtually begged her to move back to Kansas to be close to them. But in the end, she'd been reluctant to uproot Christopher from all that was familiar to him. And perhaps she hadn't really wanted to sever that last tie to Carl. She hadn't been ready to do it back then. She didn't know if she was ready even now.

"Do you have family here in the city?" he asked.

Julia pushed her thoughts away to answer his question. "My family lives on a farm just over the state line in Kansas. Christopher's paternal grandparents live about ten miles from them."

So that meant Julia had more than likely married her high-school sweetheart, Harris thought. He wondered what kind of marriage she'd had and if she'd gotten over his death. But of course he didn't know her well enough to ask her such things, even though he wished he did. "Your folks are farmers?"

She nodded. "Wheat. It's a small operation, only a few hundred acres."

His brows rose. "A few hundred acres is considered small?"

Julia laughed softly. "Yes, when you compare it to some of the other farms that have several thousand acres."

"I'm rather ignorant about farming," he said. "Dad was in the mud business and I grew up learning about that sort of thing."

"I'm finished, Mommy, see?" Christopher piped up.

Smiling indulgently, Julia reached for the small platter of brownies.

"You'd better give me one, too, Julia. Cook would be disappointed if we left any," he said as she served one of the chocolate squares to her son.

After handing the tray to Harris, she said, "I'm afraid I'm ignorant about the mud business. In fact, I've never heard of it."

"Actually it's a little more than just mud. It's a chemical mixture that's used on drilling rigs," Harris replied.

"You mean as in gas and oil?"

Nodding, he bit into the chewy brownie, then winked down the table at Christopher who was busily doing the same.

"It's used to cool the casing," he went on, "or the drilling bit as you might think of it."

Julia told herself not to be curious about the man, but each time she did, she found another question on her tongue. "That's nothing like law. What made you decide to become a judge?"

He grinned broadly. Julia Warren was beginning to thaw out. "I watched a lot of Perry Mason," he said jokingly.

An odd look of pain suddenly crossed her delicate features. Harris couldn't imagine what had put it there. "You didn't like Perry Mason?" he asked.

Silent fury choked Julia as she thought about Carl, about all she and Christopher had lost and suffered through because a judge, just like this man, hadn't done his job. She wanted to tell all that to Harris Hargrove, but she didn't. Instead, she slowly counted to ten and reminded herself that being here had nothing to do with laws or judgments.

"Perry Mason was before my time," she said, struggling to keep her voice natural.

"Well, actually he was before mine, too," Harris said with an impish grin. "But I love the reruns."

It dawned on Julia that he was only teasing her, and she felt both foolish and embarrassed about her angry thoughts. She hoped he hadn't picked up on them. He wouldn't understand why she'd had them, and she certainly had no intention of explaining anything so personal to this man.

Smiling faintly, she lifted her gaze to his. "I like the reruns, too. Only I don't imagine things go that way in a real courtroom."

He chuckled. "If only it were that cut and dried."

"I'm finished, Mommy!" Christopher declared. "Can we go outside now, please?"

Grateful for the interruption, Julia turned to her son. "If Mr. —er, Harry is finished with his lunch..."

Harris plucked another brownie from the tray. "I'll just take this with me. Let's go through the kitchen," he said as the three of them left the table. "I want you to meet Cook."

Cook turned out to be a big man somewhere in his late fifties. His rust-colored hair lay in tight waves against his head and a narrow mustache of the same color lined his upper lip.

"Julia, this is Cook. We call him that because he won't tell us what his real name is. I suspect it's Waldo—what's your guess?"

The older man gave Harris a threatening look before extending his hand to Julia. It was easy for Julia to see that the two men were more friends than employer-employee.

"My pleasure, ma'am. Harry tells me you're going to be doing Rose's birthday party."

"I hope you're not offended."

The man roared with laughter. "Me feed a hundred people? Why, I'd kick Harry in the—er, shins if he even asked. But I'll be here to help with anything you need. Looking forward to it, in fact."

"Thank you," Julia told him. "And thank you for the lunch. It was delicious. Christopher thanks you, too," she added as Cook's attention turned to her son.

"Well now, if you aren't a handsome lad. How old are you?" Cook asked.

Christopher's grin was wide. "Four! And next year I'll be in kindergarten."

Cook chuckled. "That sounds pretty old to me."

"We're going out back so Chris can meet Oscar," Harris told Cook.

"Have fun and come back to see me, Mr. Chris," the older man said.

Harris guided Julia and Chris out of the kitchen and into a room that appeared to be a den. One wall contained a set of sliding glass doors leading out to a small concrete patio. Harris pushed them aside and Christopher shot through the opening ahead of the adults.

Chapter Five

Once outside, Julia looked curiously around her. The first impression she had was one of overflowing vegetation. The same green ivy that adorned the front of the house was present here, also. It covered a trellis that shaded the west end of the patio, then traveled for several feet along the eaves beneath the roof. To the left of the patio was the rose garden she'd anticipated. At the moment the bushes were in full bloom, creating a riot of white, red, pink and yellow. The scent of the blossoms hung in the hot, humid air.

Several feet from the patio was a rectangular pool, complete with slide, diving board and outdoor furniture grouped at one end. Christopher raced toward the pool, then braked to a stop a couple of feet from the edge.

"No farther, Chris," Julia warned. "You might fall in shoes and all."

Giggling, Chris backed away, then took off in a run across the green expanse of lawn that stretched away from the house. He'd gone only a few yards when a golden Labrador bounded out of the trees and straight to him.

"I take it that's Oscar?" Julia asked as Harris walked up behind her.

Harris smiled as he watched the dog and child get acquainted. "Oscar loves children. They have much more energy to play than crotchety old judges."

Julia winced inwardly at his description. It was the same one she'd given him herself. But that was before she'd met him. Now it was more than obvious that he was young, virile and far more personable than she wanted to admit. "He's a beautiful dog. Are you an animal lover?"

Nodding, he said, "Oscar is like a companion. I'd miss him terribly if he wasn't around."

Christopher's laughter filtered to them as Oscar began to lick the child's face. For a moment Julia watched the two of them wrestle playfully on the grass and remembered back to when she was a child on the farm. Animals of all sorts had been a part of her life.

"I had a pet hog when I was small," Julia said, turning and smiling up at him. "Her name was Ginger and she was the most beautiful Duroc gilt you can imagine."

"What happened to Ginger?" he asked with amusement while his eyes drank in the vibrant color of her fiery hair, the sparkle of her smile.

"She won a blue ribbon at the county fair. Then she became a mother. After that she didn't have much time for play. But for a while we were the best of friends."

"I've heard hogs are very intelligent animals." But Harris couldn't imagine Julia with one, or even on a farm doing chores. Her regal beauty was more fitting for a model, or a princess.

"Oh, they are. I still believe Ginger understood everything I said to her, especially when I told her how pretty she was."

Harris laughed and Julia suddenly realized they were getting entirely too friendly. Her cheeks reddened as she glanced away from him and out over the perfectly manicured lawn. "Enough about that," she said. "Are you ready to show me how you want things?"

The idea of showing her what he really wanted brought an amused tilt to his lips, and he wondered what her reaction would be if he took it upon himself to kiss her.

"I'd really rather hear about you and the hog," he said teasingly.

The color in her cheeks deepened as she shook her head, glanced at him, then away again. His probing brown eyes unsettled her, especially when she felt so drawn to look into them. Julia took a deep breath. "We should really get on with things. I need to be back home before late."

"Of course," he said, then gestured at the patio and connecting lawn. "This is it. What do you think?"

Julia forced herself to think ahead to the party. "It's very beautiful. I don't foresee any problem putting the eating tables beneath the shade trees," she told him, motioning toward the open area of the lawn where Christopher and Oscar were still playing. "And the serving tables here on the patio. Is that agreeable to you?"

"Fine. As I said before, you know more about this than I do."

He was standing close beside her. Julia glanced up at him and was reminded what a big man he was. The top of her head hardly reached his shoulder. But she didn't find his height nearly as intimidating as the sex appeal he radiated.

Christopher and Oscar chose that moment to race toward the adults. Oscar barked with excitement and nipped playfully at the boy's heels. "Christopher is in heaven," Julia said. "He's begged for a dog for months now, but I haven't a place to keep one."

Boy and dog tumbled to a stop at Julia's feet. Giggling fitfully, Christopher pressed his cheek against the dog's head. "Isn't he beautiful, Mommy? See how he likes me?"

Julia smiled down at her son, but her heart squeezed with pain. There was something about this man and his dog that reminded her of all Christopher was missing because his father was gone. Forcing the thought aside, she said, "Yes, I can see he likes you. Are you ready for a swim now? We'll have to be going soon."

The smile fell from the child's face as he looked at his newfound friend. "What about Oscar? Can he swim with me?"

"I doubt—" Julia began.

"Sure he can," Harris interjected. "Oscar loves to swim."

"Yippee!" Christopher shouted happily and quickly began to shed his shirt, tennis shoes and socks.

Julia looked apologetically at Harris. "You don't have to let—"

"It's all right," he assured her before she could finish. "I let him swim with me at times. I'll just have the gardener put in extra chemical tomorrow."

Julia laughed. "I think you'd be in trouble if you had children. They'd be spoiled rotten."

Chuckling, he guided her over to the table and chairs shaded by a huge yellow-and-white umbrella. "It feels nice to be able to indulge Chris," he told her as they took a seat. "So many children come through the courts and I can't help them all. It's tragic."

There it was again, she thought. The hint of compassion in his voice, on his face. It made Julia wonder if he really did care about the cases he presided over, or was it, to him, merely a job with an impressive title?

It had never occurred to her that Harry, or any judge for that matter, might actually care about the people involved in the cases before them. She'd always thought of judges as impersonal, people who merely saw that rules and laws were followed in the courtroom no matter what the cost.

But perhaps there were judges who did care, she argued with herself in an effort to be fair. Still, she found that difficult to believe when they allowed killers to post bail and walk free....

"Come down to this end, Chris," Harris told the boy. "It's just your size."

Julia leaned back against the chair and watched Christopher splash into the shallow end of the pool. Oscar didn't need coaxing—he jumped right in behind, making the child shriek with laughter.

As the boy and dog played, a silence fell between the two adults. Julia felt herself growing tense and decided it would help if she talked. "I suppose you see and hear some horrendous things in the courtroom. Do you like your job?"

His gaze slanted over to her and Julia found herself admiring the way his black hair lay sleek and shiny against his head.

"Not very many people have asked me that question. Everyone takes it for granted that I do like it. I wonder why you didn't?"

Julia felt herself blushing and she tried to explain her question. "The law is a complex thing. It can't always be easy for you."

"It's never easy, Julia. But it's rewarding." A half grin crooked his lips. "And what about you? Do you like your job?"

She nodded as she drew an imaginary figure on the table with her finger. "I've always liked cooking, and it was something I could do without going back to college." She looked over at him, her expression wry. "I guess that sounds lazy to someone like you who spent years in school."

"No. I realize everyone is not suited or driven to earn an advanced degree. I'm probably guilty of being a lot of things, but I hope a snob is not one of them."

No, Julia didn't think he was a snob. It was one of the first things she'd noticed about him. She'd expected to go into his office and meet a person with a superior attitude. Instead, she'd found a warm, likable man.

That was something she admitted to herself reluctantly. But it wasn't right, she thought as she watched her son splash about in the pool. She shouldn't be sitting here with this man, talking so casually. He was a part of the system that had caused her husband's death. How could she forget something like that? Still, it had been so long since she'd been in a man's company that it was nice, just for a moment, to let herself believe he was simply a man and she simply a woman.

"I married right out of high school," she heard herself saying. "Soon after, I had Chris and...then my husband died. Even if I'd wanted to go to college I haven't had the time or the funds."

His eyes slipped slowly over her features, savoring every nuance. The wind teased the tiny curls framing her face, and the heat had brought a damp sheen to her pearly skin. Color stained her cheeks and the bridge of her nose. He found himself wanting to reach over and put his hand beneath her chin, draw her face up so that he could look straight into her gray eyes. "I can't imagine what that must have been like for you," he said quietly.

Julia's lips thinned with a bitterness she was afraid she was always going to carry inside. She wanted to ask him if he didn't see victims like herself in the courtroom every day. But to do that would be cracking open the door to her heart and allowing him a peek inside. She definitely didn't want that.

"Don't feel sorry for me. I have a full life."

Did she? Harris wondered. She was such a reserved woman, even though she'd smiled and laughed more than once since she'd arrived. There was something in her eyes, a haunted look he'd first noticed yesterday in his office that told him her life wasn't as complete as she tried to convey.

"I only feel sorry for people who can't change their unfortunate circumstances. And even then I don't let them know it," he told her.

She was still thinking about that when Christopher climbed out of the pool and trotted over to where she and Harris sat in the shade of the umbrella.

"Can I go down the slide?" he asked Harris. Behind him Oscar shook with a vengeance, showering the two adults.

Julia squealed with shock at the unexpected spray of cool water. Chuckling, Harris said, "Sure. And you go with him, Oscar, or I'll take you to the big tree."

The Labrador and Chris raced back to the pool. Watching them, Julia found herself smiling. "I take it the big tree is something evil," she said.

Harris laughed. "It's where Oscar's doghouse and chain are. Not one of his favorite spots. Sorry he forgot his manners."

Julia shook her head. "Don't apologize. It's so hot today, the water feels good."

His brown eyes warmed as they traveled over her. Her blouse was still splotched with water, but the drops on her skin were quickly evaporating in the heat. "You should have brought your suit and joined Chris in the pool."

"It was enough to impose Chris on you," she said. Julia couldn't imagine baring herself in a swimsuit in front of this man. It had been difficult enough just to accept his offer of lunch. She still hadn't figured out exactly why he'd offered it. There wasn't really anything left to discuss where the party was concerned, and she certainly couldn't imagine his being attracted to her. They were from entirely different circles. And from the looks of him she imagined he had his pick of women.

"It was no imposition. I love children. Even my sister's stepchildren who happen to be little monsters," he said with a wry grimace.

This brought a smile to Julia's lips. "Chris can be a monster, too."

"They all are sometimes," he said. "Is it difficult for you, raising him alone?"

The question was personal, but coming from Harris it seemed even more so. "Only at times. But I know that will change when he gets older and enters high school. When that time comes I only hope I can make the right decisions as a parent."

Harris couldn't imagine her staying single for that long. She was so lovely and he was certain that underneath that auburn hair and ivory skin was a passionate woman. She would have so much to give a man that it seemed almost a sacrilege for her to remain alone.

Julia shifted her eyes back to Christopher, but her mind was on Harris. She wondered why he wasn't married. Most men his age were, or at least had been at one time.

Harris, on the other hand, was thinking of the many times he'd agonized over making the right decision about a man, or woman, or child. Someone who had somewhere along the way stumbled and staggered onto the wrong side of the law. It was as he'd told Julia—never cut and dried. Nor hardly ever as simple as guilty or not. Sometimes he thought no one really knew or understood the heavy weight of responsibility on his shoulders. And he knew that his life had come down to that of being a judge and nothing else. Looking at Julia, he realized it more than ever.

Christopher swam for a few more minutes and Harris went in to have Cook fix them something cool to drink.

Minutes later, when the older man arrived on the patio with a tray, Julia ordered the boy out of the pool and dried him with a towel Cook had thoughtfully provided.

"You can't have lemonade, Oscar," Harris said as the dog looked expectantly up at the three sitting around the table. "Go dry yourself off. Where are your manners?"

The dog barked, then turned and ran across the lawn to a chosen spot where he shook, then rolled with exuberance over the grass.

"Oscar is funny," Christopher said, giggling.

"Oscar is mischievous," Harris said. "Sometimes he gets into trouble."

"That's what Mommy says I am," Christopher told him.

Harris laughed and it was plain to Julia that this man, the judge, truly enjoyed being with her son. The knowledge confused her, but then the whole afternoon confused her.

"You know what, Harry?" Christopher continued, realizing he had an audience in his new friend. "I have a parrot. Her name is Josephine."

"That sounds interesting. Can she talk?" Harris asked.

Christopher nodded proudly. "She can say my name and a bunch of words. She likes to watch TV, too. Would you like to come to my house and see her?"

Julia, who'd just taken a drink of lemonade, nearly sprayed a mouthful across the table. Her hand went to her throat and she swallowed with difficulty.

Harris watched her, wondering if she would have the same reaction if Christopher had issued the same invitation to some other man. He'd never thought of himself as a ladies' man, but he'd never thought of himself as repulsive, either. He wondered what it was about him that Julia Warren didn't like.

"I'd love to see her. But I'm afraid I can't today," he told the boy. "Maybe soon."

"Tomorrow?"

"Harry has to work, Chris," Julia said, finding her voice.

Christopher's head sank dejectedly and Julia felt a little ashamed of herself. Christopher was so hungry for male companionship. And she wanted him to have it. But not with this man!

Harris reached over and ruffled the boy's tawny head. "Tell you what, Chris. The next time I can find a little spare time, I'll come by, if your mother doesn't mind."

Christopher's eyes flew eagerly to his mother. "He can, can't he, Mommy?"

Oh, how had she gotten herself into this? she wondered wildly. "Er, well, I guess so. If Mr.—if Harry would like to."

Christopher beamed happily. "See, Harry, she don't mind at all."

Harris somehow rather doubted Julia was that receptive to the idea, but he wasn't going to complain. At least she hadn't refused him the invitation outright.

Julia hurriedly began to gather up her purse and Christopher's things. "I think we'd better be going," she told Harris. "I'm sure you're a busy man and I have work waiting for me at home."

He smiled easily at her, while silently noting her nervous movements. "I understand. And I'm grateful that you had time to come look the place over. As I said before, I know nothing about parties, and I didn't really know how appropriate this place could be."

"It'll be lovely. I'm sure your mother will be pleasantly surprised." Julia got up from the table and went around to start tying the first of Christopher's untied tennis shoes.

Before she was aware that he'd moved, Harris kneeled down beside her and began tying the other shoe. It put him very close to Julia. So close that she could smell the subtle scent of his cologne. She could feel the heat of his body, and from the corner of her eye she could see his arm, so dark and strong and masculine. She could almost imagine the feel of it around her shoulder or curved around her waist.

The erotic thought was unexpected and disturbed her greatly. She quickly finished tying the shoe and rose to her feet.

"There you go, sport," Harris said after he'd finished tying the other shoe. "You're all ready now."

Julia glanced at him as they walked across the patio. "Thank you for being so helpful with Christopher," she said.

Harris looked at her and smiled. "Christopher has been a joy." And so had she, he thought, but stopped himself short of saying so aloud. Somehow he knew that even the slightest overture from him would turn Julia Warren into an iceberg.

Out on the driveway Harris lifted Christopher into the passenger seat while Julia climbed behind the wheel.

"I like your house and your swimming pool, Harry," Christopher told him. "Can I come back and see you again?"

Christopher was looking eagerly out the open window at Harris.

"I hope you will, Chris. Goodbye." He looked across to Julia.

Twin spots of red stained her cheeks, but her eyes met his frankly and for a moment he was taken with their gray clarity. "And I'll see you at the party, Julia."

The party. For a moment her mind had to struggle to remember why she was here in the first place. "Y-yes," she finally stammered. "I'll see you at the party. Goodbye."

Quickly she started the engine and slipped the van into gear. Harris stepped back, and with great relief she pulled away and headed down the drive that would lead them out of the estate.

Chapter Six

Julia checked the thermometer on the big iron smoker and decided it needed a couple of more sticks of hickory to hold the fire until three in the morning. At that time the alarm would wake her so that she could check the fire again.

Good brisket and ribs took long hours of simmering over a bed of hickory coals. She'd had a huge cooker especially made so that large amounts of meat could be prepared at one time. It was Saturday night and the beef for Harry's party was beginning to cook and spit over the hot coals. Tomorrow she'd add the chickens, which cooked much more quickly than the beef.

"How does it look?"

Julia looked over her shoulder at the sound of Rhonda's voice. "Good. I'm going to check it at three. What did you decide about the sauce? Do you think we have enough?"

The women made their own special barbecue sauce. It had become a trademark of sorts among their customers and to run short at the Hargrove party would be nothing short of a catastrophe.

Rhonda nodded. "Plenty."

"What about the corn and the new potatoes?"

"It looks like a truck patch in the kitchen right now," Rhonda said, then glanced at her watch. "It's ten. Are you ready to quit for the night?"

Julia stared at her partner as if she'd lost her mind. "Quit? We have more than a hundred ears of corn to husk. We can't get everything ready tomorrow. Not when we're going to have to make an extra trip to Harry's just for the dishes and cutlery."

Rhonda grinned. "So we're calling the man Harry now. That lunch you had with him the other day must have been pretty intimate."

Julia's face registered complete surprise. She hadn't realized she'd even said Harry. But it shouldn't surprise her that much. All week, since she and Christopher had visited his place, she'd thought of him as Harry. Worse than that, she'd thought of him almost continually.

More cross at herself than at Rhonda's remark, she turned away from the cooker and headed toward the workroom. Rhonda followed right on her heels.

"It wasn't intimate, for Pete's sake," Julia told her as they entered the cool, air-conditioned kitchen. "Christopher was with me. You know that."

"Yes, but that's just about all I know. Every time I ask you about it, you clam up."

Julia moved over to several boxes of fresh corn stacked in one corner of the room. "That's not true," she said, not bothering to look up at Rhonda. "I told you everything about the place."

Rhonda made a sound of impatience as she reached to help Julia lift a box of corn onto a work table. "I'm not interested in the *place*. I want to hear about the *man*. What did you two talk about?"

Julia shrugged and carefully avoided Rhonda's gaze. Talking about Harry made her nervous, and she didn't want her friend to pick up on just how nervous.

"Nothing in particular. Just the party and what needed to be done for it. Besides, Chris talked the man's ear off."

"I gathered that Chris liked him a lot. He told me all about him."

Julia looked at her friend. "I didn't realize he'd even mentioned the outing to you."

"Oh, he did all right. He says that Harry is going to come see his parrot. Is that true?"

Julia felt her cheeks fill with heat. "I rather doubt it. I think he only told Christopher that to pacify him."

"You mean that's what you're hoping he was doing," Rhonda said slyly.

Julia made a face and picked up one of the green corn ears. "Quit trying to make something out of nothing. The man is merely our client, nothing more." She began to yank the tough husks away from the yellow corn and toss the waste aside. "Besides, you of all people know I would never look twice at a judge."

But she had looked twice, she thought miserably. And she'd certainly thought about him more than twice. She'd thought of him all week and wondered what he'd been doing, the cases he'd been working on and if he thought about her. It was insane, she knew. But she hadn't been able to stop herself.

Rhonda reached for an ear of corn and quickly began to husk it. "He's not just a judge. He's also a man."

"For me it would be impossible to separate the two," Julia said grimly.

"Well I, for one, can't wait to meet the man in person. It's always exciting to meet a man with authority."

Julia rolled her eyes. "Why should his authority make him any more exciting than the next man?"

Rhonda's eyes took on a wicked gleam. "There's something about a man with a lot of power. It makes them much sexier."

If Harris T. Hargrove was any sexier he'd need to order himself locked up for being armed and extremely dangerous, Julia thought.

"So you say," Julia responded, purposely sounding bored.

"What are we going to wear tomorrow night? Jeans?" Rhonda asked.

Julia wrinkled her nose. "I thought our blue shifts and white ruffled aprons would look nice."

Rhonda's brows lifted. "My, my, you are going all out for this one, aren't you?"

Julia grimaced, annoyed that Rhonda persisted with the subject of Harris T. Hargrove. "I'm only talking about wearing simple cotton dresses. Nothing special."

"I thought this was going to be a casual affair?"

Julia kept her eyes on the corn in her hands. "It is. But as *you* keep reminding me, these people are in a higher social circle. I don't want us to appear frumpy. It wouldn't be good for business."

Rhonda didn't say anything, and when Julia finally looked up she saw a knowing grin on her friend's face.

"Uh-huh," Rhonda drawled. "I just wonder if it's the business you're really concerned about."

From out of nowhere a streak of mischief hit Julia. Before she realized what she was doing she threw the corn husks she was holding straight at Rhonda, who ducked but not quickly enough. A wad of corn silks smacked her in the middle of the forehead and caught in her bangs.

Julia's giggles started slowly, then grew to outright laughter as Rhonda peered through the tassels of corn silk.

"That's what you get for making insinuations," Julia said between bursts of laughter.

Rhonda reached up and jerked the sticky silks from her face and hair. Before Julia guessed her intention, she threw them back at her. Soon the two women were in an all-out war of husks. Green leaves and yellow silks flew through the air and littered half the kitchen.

"My Lord, look what we've done," Rhonda said with dismay after they'd both surrendered. "It's going to take us an hour to clean up this mess!"

Julia didn't care. At least the playful little war had taken her mind off Harris and the party for a few minutes.

Grinning, she reached up and brushed a few stray corn silks from Rhonda's dark hair. "Maybe you won't accuse me of having eyes for Judge Hargrove after this."

"I'll hold my opinion until tomorrow night at the party," Rhonda returned.

Julia's expression suddenly became closed, and she bent down to pick up handfuls of husk.

The smile fell from Rhonda's face as she watched Julia's wooden movements. "I was only kidding, honey."

"I know," Julia murmured, her head still bent as she continued to pick up the mess scattered across the floor.

"Well, you don't have to go cold on me," Rhonda said.

Julia glanced up at her friend. "I'm not cold. I'm just sort of... anxious, that's all."

Rhonda squatted down beside Julia and began to help her clean away the corn husks. "There's nothing to be anxious about, Julia. We've done parties far fancier than this one. Remember that politician that wanted the flambé chicken? This party will be a snap compared to that one."

Julia forced a smile. "Oh, I know. It's just the man," she said, suddenly deciding to be honest with Rhonda.

"What about him, other than the fact that he's a judge?"

"He scares me."

Rhonda leaned back and studied her redheaded friend quizzically. "Scares you? Whyever would he scare you?"

"I don't know. Maybe it's that authority you were talking about. And I keep wondering what Carl would think about my working for a judge."

"Carl's opinions shouldn't matter, Julia. He's gone. He'll never come back and you'll never have a life of your own again if you keep trying to cling to him."

"I'm not trying to cling to him," Julia denied.

Rhonda didn't argue the point; she didn't have to. The look she gave Julia said she didn't believe her for a minute.

"Come on," Julia said, changing the subject. "Let's get to work. We've got a lot more corn to husk. At this rate I won't need the alarm to wake me at three. I'll still be up."

Sunday dawned clear and warm. By seven Julia and Rhonda were back in the kitchen, and they worked steadily throughout the day. By three o'clock that afternoon the food was under control and the dishes and cutlery loaded into the van.

Julia called Michelle, a high school student who lived across the street, to come over and baby-sit Christopher.

After giving the girl the usual last-minute instructions, Julia hurried back outside where Rhonda was waiting in the van with the motor already running.

"We'd better shake a leg, girl, if we're going to get there and back here in time to change our clothes and get the food loaded," Rhonda said as Julia climbed into the passenger seat.

"I know," Julia agreed, leaning back to catch her breath. "But Harry's cook said he'd be glad to help, so maybe he'll give us a hand setting up the tables."

When they arrived at the Hargrove estate, Cook was more than glad to help, and he immediately began to assist in unloading the van. He said that Harris had run across town to do a last-minute errand.

Julia breathed easier after hearing the news and was able to concentrate on the work to be done without worrying about running into Harry. By the time she and Rhonda left the estate, potted plants and clusters of balloons decorated the patio, swimming pool and lawn. Beneath the shade of the oaks, the tables were set with gleaming dishes. All that was needed now was the food and the guests.

When the two women arrived back at their work room, they quickly loaded the food into warmers built into the back of the van, then went to their respective houses to shower and change.

The day had grown very hot, so Julia pinned her hair into a French twist. It would be cooler that way.

"Mommy, I wish I could go to Harry's party."

In her mirror Julia saw Christopher standing in the doorway of the bedroom. Her heart softened at the sight of his glum expression.

"I know, honey, but this party is only for big people. Maybe you can go to the next party we do."

His bottom lip quivered. "But Harry won't be at the next one."

Julia had to stifle a groan. The man had not only managed to leave an impression on her, but on her son, too.

She crossed the room and knelt down in front of him. "Did you like Harry that much?"

Christopher nodded emphatically and Julia felt her heart sink. In spite of her better judgment, she'd liked the man, too. And if she was honest with herself, she had to admit that she was looking forward to seeing him again tonight.

"Well, I tell you what, Chris. I'll make it a point to tell him that, okay? Maybe he'll come by and see Josephine."

"Do you think so?" Christopher asked hopefully.

Julia hoped not, but she couldn't bear to see Christopher disappointed. If seeing Harry again meant that much to him, then she could live through one little visit.

Julia reached out and touched his nose with the tip of her finger. "Maybe," she told him, then kissed him twice on the cheek. "Now go get Michelle to read you a story and I'll be back before you know it."

Christopher got as far as the hallway, then turned back to his mother. "Don't forget to tell him, Mommy."

"I won't," Julia said, smiling. How could she forget? she thought. She never seemed to stop thinking about the man. She wondered desperately how she was going to manage to get through the evening ahead.

Harry had said a hundred guests would be attending the party, but Julia and Rhonda estimated there were at least twenty-five more than that. Thankfully, as usual, they'd allowed for extras.

The sun was still blazing in the western sky when they arranged the food on the buffet tables on the patio, but the shade beneath the ivy-covered trellis was cool and deep. Most of the guest were milling there; others had ventured out onto the lawn and were gathered in clusters under the trees there.

Rhonda, Julia and Cook had passed around drinks of fruit punch, coffee and iced tea to keep everyone pacified until the finishing touches could be put on the buffet tables. So far, Julia hadn't seen Harry, and she wondered if he was still out running his errand. Surely judges weren't called out on Sunday nights, were they?

"Everything is beautiful, ladies. If it tastes as good as it looks I can't wait."

Julia looked up to see the very person she'd been thinking about standing directly across the table from her and Rhonda. Seeing Harry again, especially so close, took her breath away.

He was wearing a pair of jeans and a simple pocket T-shirt the color of a ripe melon, but the very casual clothes had nothing to do with the way his appearance affected her. It was the man himself.

"I don't think you'll be disappointed," she murmured, unaware of the shy smile touching her lips. She glanced at Rhonda, who was busily eyeing Harris.

"Rhonda, this is Judge Hargrove, the man who is paying us for all this work."

Rhonda's eyes widened and she cast a knowing little look Julia's way before she extended a hand to Harris. "Hello. I'm Rhonda Genoa. It's very nice to finally meet you in person, Judge. Thank you for giving us the chance to do this party."

Harry waved away her thanks. "No thanks are needed. You came highly recommended."

He looked back at Julia who was absently fidgeting with a relish tray. "How's Chris?"

Julia's gaze met his. She wondered if he was feeling the same jolt of electricity she was. "He's very well, thank you."

"And you?"

Why was he doing this? Why didn't he move away and mingle with his guests?

"I—I've been fine, too," she said jerkily, knowing Rhonda was watching like a hawk.

"That's good," he said.

He kept standing there as if he expected something else from her. When it didn't come he asked, "How long until the guests can eat?"

"If you'd like to get the crowd's attention, I think things are ready now," Rhonda said.

"Fine. I'll go get the guest of honor," he said with a lazy smile and left them.

As Julia watched him walk away, a pent-up breath whooshed out of her.

"My God, what's wrong with you, Julia? You look like you've fallen into a flour barrel!"

Julia lifted a shaky hand to her cheek. Was she really pale? "Nothing's wrong," she told Rhonda. "I'm just hot. The humidity is terrible tonight."

Across the lawn Harry was leaning over an elegant gray-headed lady sitting in a webbed lawn chair. Julia watched as he said something in her ear, then kissed her cheek. The woman gazed at him fondly and laughed.

"You didn't tell me that Harris T. Hargrove looked like that!" Rhonda said in hushed tones.

"Why should I discuss his looks?" Julia said a little crossly. "They have nothing to do with me."

"Nor me, either, apparently," Rhonda muttered.

"What does that mean?" Julia asked.

"It's obvious the man has eyes only for you. You didn't tell me that, either."

"The heat must be getting to you, too," Julia mumbled, glad to see the guests were now approaching the tables to serve themselves.

"I'm going in to see if Cook was able to find any more crushed ice," she told Rhonda, and hurried into the house.

For the next hour Julia carried food from the kitchen to the patio to replenish the dishes the guests quickly devoured. Eventually their appetites seemed to wane, and Julia decided she'd take a break before it was time to serve dessert.

She found the kitchen empty. The silence was quite a contrast to all the talk and laughter outside. Someone had set up a CD player and many couples were dancing on the concrete patio surrounding the swimming pool.

"So here you are. Why don't you bring your drink outside with the rest of us?"

Julia had been in the process of filling a glass with ice and tea. At the unexpected sound of Harris's voice she turned with a start. "Oh, I didn't realize you were here."

He walked farther into the room, his eyes quietly admiring her slim figure in the dark blue dress. "I've been looking for you. I'd like you to meet my mother."

Julia looked at him and felt her heart begin to pound erratically. "I—I'm sure your mother isn't interested in meeting me."

"Quite the opposite. I think she wants your secret recipe for the barbecue sauce," he said with a smile. "Of course you don't have to give her the original. Maybe something close to it."

She swirled the contents of her glass, making the crushed ice tinkle. "I'd be happy for her to have the recipe, but she'd better get it from Rhonda—she's better at remembering ingredients than I am."

He frowned, knowing she was putting him off. "Rhonda's busy dancing with Cook."

"Dancing? You're kidding, I hope!"

Harris laughed at her stunned expression. "No. What's wrong with her dancing?"

"Rhonda is not a guest. I'm sorry if she's forgotten her place. I'll go have a word with her if you'd like."

He reached out and took hold of her bare arm. "What a little worrier you are. Whyever would I want you to do such a thing? I'm the one who told Rhonda to join in the fun. And so should you. Besides, I think Cook would murder you. He thinks your partner is quite a dame."

"Quite a dame?" she repeated, amused in spite of the heat his fingers were spreading through her body.

He looked down at her as they walked through the house. His hand was still on her arm and her skin felt like dewy satin beneath his fingers. He wondered if the rest of her would feel as soft. "Cook has a thing for Bogart movies," he explained. "I think he likes to pretend he's living in that era."

"I see," she said with a little laugh, then darted a glance up at him. He seemed even taller than she remembered and she noticed his dark hair had grown a little since she'd last seen him. A stray lock had fallen across his forehead. At the moment, Julia thought he looked more like a rake than a judge. "Christopher wanted to come tonight. He likes you very much. I promised him I'd tell you that for him."

"I wish you'd consider bringing him over again. Usually when I'm with children it's under difficult circumstances. Your son was a lift for my spirits."

He opened the patio door and Julia stepped out into the humid night. Lanterns had been hung to ward off the darkness. Shafts of soft yellow light rippled across the swimming pool, and the smell of roses hung heavily in the air.

Julia had to admit it was a romantic night, and she was even more aware of it as Harris put his hand against her back and began to guide her through the crowd.

Mrs. Hargrove was sitting near the pool with a man and two other women. When Harry approached with Julia beside him, she looked up with interest.

"Mother, you've been wanting to meet Julia. So here she is."

Mrs. Hargrove was dressed casually in slacks and a sleeveless blouse yet still managed to look elegant. Her gray hair was cut in a short bob, and even in the darkness Julia could see that her skin was flawless. Precious stones glittered on her hand as she reached out for Julia's.

"Lovely food, dear. Everyone has been raving about it," she said.

Julia was surprised at the English accent threaded through Mrs. Hargrove's speech. She would have expected the woman to have lost it by now. "Thank you, Mrs. Hargrove. I hope you enjoyed it."

"Frightfully so, I'm afraid. I'll have to exercise for a week to get this off." She laughed and patted her flat stomach. "You know this party was really a big surprise. I thought Harry had invited me over for a spot of tea and a movie on the VCR. He fooled me." She looked at her son with great affection, then back to Julia. "Harry tells me you have an adorable son."

"That's because he saw Chris on one of his good days," Julia said, attempting to joke. Actually Mrs. Hargrove's remark had momentarily shocked her. It was hard to believe that Harris had mentioned her and Chris to his mother.

"Another song is starting," Harry said. "Why don't we go dance, Julia?"

His suggestion caught Julia completely off guard. "I, well, your mother wants the sauce recipe," she finally managed to say.

Rose Hargrove waved away Julia's words. "Oh, you go ahead, dear, and dance with Harry. He doesn't get to do nearly enough of that sort of thing. You can leave the recipe with Cook later."

"But I..."

Julia didn't have a chance to finish. Harris was already tugging her away. "Don't argue," he said. "Surely you don't have anything against one little dance," he teased.

Julia felt every nerve in her body coil tighter at the thought of being in his arms. "It's been years since I've danced. I've forgotten how," she said lamely.

They reached the far end of the pool, which was deserted at the moment except for the two of them. Before Julia could think of a way to escape, Harris took hold of her hand and drew her into his arms.

The music was slow, bluesy and easy to dance to, but Julia was barely aware of it. Harris's large hand engulfed hers and his shoulder beneath her own hand felt infinitely masculine. It had been a long time since she'd touched a man in any capacity, and it had been even longer since one had affected her as much as this one.

"You don't have to tiptoe around me just because I'm a judge. You look as if I'm going to sentence you instead of dance with you."

Julia knew he probably thought her strange. Perhaps even prudish, but she couldn't change the way she was. Men were not a part of her life. And certainly not good-looking judges.

"Sorry. Am I stepping on your toes?" she asked.

He grinned down at her. "No, you're standing a mile away from me."

The arm he had around her waist drew her closer and Julia was forced to rest her cheek against his shoulder. Beneath his clothes his muscles were rock hard and no doubt powerful. She could smell the faint scent of cologne clinging to his shirt and the unique scent of his skin.

As they moved ever so slowly to the music, his thighs brushed against hers, and Julia was afraid she was going to stop breathing all together.

"The night has turned out very hot," he remarked.

"Yes, and very humid," Julia replied.

"Still, it's a lovely night. Especially since I'm not inside reading over a case."

"Your job must keep you very busy," she commented.

"The courts are overloaded," he said, then asked, "Do you often work at night?"

His fingers threaded themselves between hers and Julia unconsciously closed her eyes at the intimate feeling. "It...varies," she said, hoping she didn't sound as breathless as she felt.

"I've thought about you and Chris this week."

Julia's eyes flew open at the unexpected words. "I can't imagine why. You must see hundreds of people throughout the week."

"That doesn't mean I remember all of them."

He was telling her he had remembered her. She didn't really know how she felt about that. The woman in her melted a little at the idea, but the part of her that resented what he stood for quickly hardened the unexpected feeling.

"Why has it been years since you danced?" he asked.

"I'm not a partyer."

She was young and beautiful. He couldn't imagine her not attending a social function once in a while. "Neither am I. Never was really. I've always filled my time with sports or law."

What about women? she wondered. Surely he made time in his life for a female or two. A man that looked like him couldn't avoid women entirely. "Well, you've danced somewhere along the way," she remarked, "because you obviously know how."

He chuckled softly. "Well, naturally I had to do a bit of dancing in my college days."

Harvard, she thought wryly. While she'd been a girl growing up on a Kansas wheat farm, he'd been in New England with the Ivy League crowd. Their lives were worlds apart. So why should it feel so wonderful to be held against him this way? she asked herself.

"Are you going to be hearing the tax-evasion trial that's rocked our local politics?" she asked.

"No. That will be heard in federal court. Besides, I know the man."

Julia lifted her head and looked at him. "Have you ever had to sentence a friend?"

He shook his head. "I would pull myself off the case if a friend was involved."

How convenient, she thought. It would have been nice if Carl had possessed that much clout. There'd been several times he'd had to arrest acquaintances. It would have made it much easier for him if he'd been able to back away and let some other officer take over.

The music was coming to an end. Julia said, "Do you think everyone is ready for dessert now?"

Harris wanted to dance with her again, but it was obvious she had other things on her mind. Still, if the evening hadn't been growing late he might have pushed for another dance.

"If you're sure you wouldn't like another dance," he murmured.

Another dance? This one had already left her insides trembling like a leaf. She'd never make it through another one. "Er, no. I should go get things ready."

Before he could say more, Julia pulled away from him and headed toward the house.

Minutes later Julia and Rhonda rolled the four-tiered birthday cake out onto the patio. The crowd oohed and aahed at the rows of flickering candles. Especially Rose Hargrove, who raised herself on tiptoe to kiss her son's cheek.

"What other son would make such a fuss over his old mum?" she asked affectionately.

Harris laughed. "You're still a pretty good ole gal, even if you have been fifty-nine for the past three years."

Everyone who'd crowded around the guest of honor hooted with laughter. Rose playfully swatted Harris's shoulder, then drew a deep breath to blow out the candles.

"Make a wish, Rose," someone in the crowd called.

Julia, who was standing just outside the group, quickly made a wish of her own. She wished she'd never met Harris T. Hargrove. Because now that she was beginning to know him she was beginning to like him, and that was going to make it difficult to forget him.

Chapter Seven

"Boy, am I ever tired," Rhonda said a few hours later as they loaded the van to go home.

"I thought you wanted to dance some more," Julia returned.

Rhonda groaned. "I don't think I could put two good steps together. But I did enjoy it. And it was so nice of the judge to invite us to join the party." She sighed contentedly and looked at Julia. "I saw you dancing with him. You didn't seem as though you were being held against your will."

Julia frowned. "Well, believe me, I was. I haven't danced since high school. It made me feel foolish."

In silent agreement, the two of them started back to the house to get the last boxes waiting on the steps. All the guests had left at least an hour ago and Harris hadn't yet returned from driving his mother home. Julia was glad. Now that the party was over, she was determined to put the man out of her mind.

Rhonda clucked her tongue. "There's lots of things you haven't done since high school. I hate to say this, Julia, but Carl really didn't give you much attention. You rarely did anything together."

"That's not true!" Julia spluttered defensively. "We did lots of things together."

"Like what?"

"Well, I don't know . . . like the police officers' annual picnic. Carl always took me to that."

"Big deal. Once a year you went to the park and ran in the sack race."

Julia's lips thinned to a grim line as they picked up the last bit of odds and ends to be loaded into the van. Was Rhonda right? While she'd been married to Carl she never really thought of herself as being neglected. He'd worked hard and put a roof over her head and food on the table. But had he really given her that much of himself?

"Just because Carl didn't take me out dancing didn't mean he wasn't a good husband," Julia said a moment later.

"I know. But he should have."

"And Bobby should have done a lot of things for you, too. Like be faithful," Julia said wryly.

"Men," Rhonda muttered. "Why do we think they're so wonderful?"

Why, indeed? Julia thought as she looked up to see Harry's BMW coming around the curve in the drive. He brought the car to a stop a few feet behind them and hopped out as though he had energy left to burn.

"You nearly missed us, Judge," Rhonda told him. "We're packed and ready to leave."

"I'm glad I didn't. It's so late I insist on seeing you safely home. It's the least I can do to express my gratitude for such a wonderful party."

"Thank you, Judge," Rhonda said before Julia could even open her mouth. "I imagine you know better than anyone that women need to be extra careful traveling across the city at night."

Julia frowned at her partner. Why couldn't she have kept her mouth shut? Now Harry was certain to escort them home. "We've never had trouble of any sort," Julia felt compelled to say.

"And that's the way we want it to stay," he said, putting an end to the subject.

"You're awfully quiet," Rhonda commented a few minutes later. "Is something wrong?"

They were driving down a four-lane boulevard that was usually very busy during the day. At this late hour, however, traffic was minimal, except for Harris's white BMW shadowing their van. Just the sight of it in the side mirror unnerved Julia.

"I'm trying to figure out why you encouraged Harry to escort us home. I really think you did it out of mischief."

"Mischief?" Rhonda repeated innocently. "Mischief had nothing to do with it. What woman in her right mind wouldn't want to be protected by a strong man like Harry?"

Julia kept her remarks to herself. To say anything else would probably only make matters worse. But during the thirty-minute drive home she crossed and recrossed her legs a number of times and drummed her fingers on the armrest.

Once they arrived at the work kitchen, Rhonda backed the van up to the door to make unloading easier.

Julia climbed out and saw Harry parking the BMW to the side of the curb. After a moment he cut the engine and lights. It looked as though he wasn't planning on going straight home, she thought with a sinking feeling.

"Oh, I'm glad you're here," Rhonda said to him as he approached. "Would you care to help Julia get this stuff back in the kitchen? On the drive over I developed an awful headache."

Julia stared openmouthed at her friend. "You didn't say anything about a headache."

Rhonda waved a hand dismissingly. "That's because I knew you'd insist on sending me into the house, and I didn't want to leave you with all this work."

Julia didn't believe her for one minute, but she certainly couldn't say anything in front of Harry.

"Of course I'd be glad to help," he said. "It's no bother at all, believe me." He threw a glance at Julia. She was fidgeting with a loose tendril of hair at the back of her neck and refused to look at him. He was beginning to wonder if he'd said or done something wrong. She hadn't been this cool the day she and Christopher had lunched with him, but it was obvious she was doing her best to avoid him now.

"You're a peach, Judge. Thanks." Rhonda quickly started across the yard to the house next door. Julia's eyes darted to Harry.

"Sorry about this. If you need to go, don't worry about it. There's really not that much to do tonight, anyway," she told him, hoping against hope he'd change his mind and leave. As it was, her heart was hammering at the thought of being alone with him.

"Nonsense. Just show me what to do," he insisted.

Julia could see he wasn't going to leave, so she opened the door to the workshop and flipped on the overhead lights.

For the next ten minutes he helped her carry in boxes and put the leftover perishables back into the refrigerator.

"This is quite a place you have here," he said, once they'd finished putting the last of the things away. Standing in the middle of the room, his thumbs hooked over the back pockets of his jeans, he took a slow survey of the room. "How long have you had it?"

Julia leaned her hip against one of the tables. Since they'd been working together the past few minutes, she'd lost some of her earlier tenseness. It was crazy for her to be edgy around the man, anyway, she told herself. He was just an ordinary guy who banged a wooden gavel and said, "Be seated, please." At least it made her feel better to think that.

"About three and a half years."

He looked surprised. "Surely you've catered longer than that?"

She shook her head. "I didn't start catering until shortly after my husband died."

"And you've already built a name for yourself here in the city. That's impressive."

She warmed to his compliment. "I don't know if we really have that much of a name yet. But thank you. It's been a hard climb at times. And there's still a long way to go. We're thinking about hiring a couple of helpers and expanding. Someday we'd like to have a whole staff of cooks and helpers."

"Sounds ambitious." He brought his dark roaming gaze to a halt on her, and Julia fought the urge to squirm beneath it.

"And expensive," she added.

He shoved his hands into his pockets and let out a long breath. He knew it was time to go. He was stalling and she probably knew it. "You've made it this far. There's no reason to think you can't make it the rest of the way."

Julia glanced down and moistened her dry lips with the tip of her tongue. It was getting late. But it would seem rude of her to send him way without offering him something to drink. He'd gone out of his way to help her. Most people she worked for were demanding instead of helpful. "Er, would you like to come into the house for a cup of coffee?"

Her suggestion took him by surprise. It must have shown on his face, because she laughed softly and said, "I know it's a late hour for coffee, but I'm one of those strange people who use it to unwind."

Harris wasn't one to argue when good fortune fell in his lap. "Coffee sounds good. Lead the way."

He followed her out of the building and across the small backyard. It was bordered with clipped hedges, and in one corner there was a gym set with a sandpile beside it.

They stepped onto a small porch, and Julia opened a door that led directly into the kitchen.

"I'll just go tell the sitter she can go home," Julia tossed over her shoulder. "Make yourself at home."

Harris watched her slender figure disappear through a door, then took a seat at the maple kitchen table. He could hear muffled voices coming from another part of the house. No doubt Julia was making sure her son was all right.

While he waited for her to return, his eyes made a slow perusal of the room. It was small, but neat and homey. On the cabinet counter was a ceramic pink pig that was more than likely stuffed with cookies. The curtains at the windows were in red-and-blue checks and bordered with farm animals.

On the table in front of him were two little pink pigs used as salt and pepper shakers. A woven basket lined with quilted calico was piled high with dinner rolls. The kitchen was far more feminine than his, he decided. Cook kept everything clinically bare. Which was fine, but this room invited a person to sit down and relax.

Footsteps sounded on the tile and he glanced around to see Julia entering the kitchen. She was pulling the pins from her hair. As she walked, the mass of red curls tumbled onto her shoulders.

Harry found the sight erotic, even though they were in a brightly lit kitchen and both fully dressed. She was a sensual woman; from the vibrant color of her hair to the way she moved. He wondered if she was even aware of it.

"I have soda or fruit juice if you prefer," she said as she got busy filling the coffeemaker with cold water.

"Coffee is fine."

She finished her preparations and flipped on the brew switch. Once it started to drip into the glass carafe, she reached to remove the small white apron she'd tied at the back of her dress. The ends had somehow tightened into a knot. As she fumbled with it, she looked at him and smiled a bit nervously. "The baby-sitter was sound asleep. I had to wake her."

"And Chris?"

"Oh, he's always asleep by nine." She finally managed to untie the apron. Tossing it aside, she glanced back at the coffeemaker. She could feel Harry's eyes on her, and the knowledge made her feel hot one second and breathless the next.

Harry leaned back in his chair and thrust his fingers through his dark hair. "I don't think I could manage this party stuff too often. It's more work than I thought."

"You must have lots of friends. All of them, and more, showed up tonight."

He chuckled softly. "I have a few. But I imagine I have more enemies. Being a judge doesn't always make you the most popular guy in the world."

Julia felt a stab of guilt. She, too, had set out to dislike him because he was a judge. About everything else Julia didn't have a prejudiced bone in her body, but his being a part of the judicial system hit too close to the heart.

"No, I suppose not," she replied. Feeling suddenly nervous again, she began to take cups and saucers down from the cabinet. It had been a long time since a man had been in her house. Oh, since Carl's death there'd been the occasional male visitor, but he'd either been family or a harmless old friend. Harris fell far short of either category.

The coffeemaker gave its last gurgle. She quickly filled a couple of cups and carried them to the table, then took a seat at the corner next to him. To sit on the opposite end of the table would have looked ridiculous.

"I'm glad you asked me in tonight, Julia."

Her heart did a little flip and she brought her gaze up to his. "Oh?"

Her face wore such a look of apprehension that he felt the need to reassure her. Quickly he reached over and touched her fingers. "Don't look so frightened."

She forced a light laugh, but her eyes darted away from his. "I—I'm not frightened. Why should I be?"

He shrugged. "I don't know. But I was getting the feeling that I make you edgy."

"Edgy" wasn't the word for it, she thought. "Nonsense. If—if I seem that way it's only because I'm tired."

His brown eyes studied the elegant lines of her face and throat. "I'm glad," he said softly, "because I'd like to see you again."

She looked at him and he watched her gray eyes darken with an emotion he couldn't quite read. He wished more than anything that he knew what she was feeling.

"I'm sorry, but I can't."

Her words were clipped and cool. She lowered her gaze, then pulled her fingers away from his and quickly lifted her cup to her lips.

Harry's expression was quizzical as he watched her. "Well, you certainly don't lead a man on, do you?"

She shook her head. "I don't. Please don't take it personally."

He laughed as though he found her words incredible. "How else could I take it, Julia?"

Her gaze returned to his face. Lord, he was so good to look at. So strong and masculine. Something about him pulled at her, and the pull was so strong it frightened her. "It's not you. I don't go out with men. Period. There's no place for a man in my life."

"I understand that you're a widow. But he's been dead for several years."

Julia felt both foolish and furious at his words. He didn't understand. How could he?

"Yes," she said, her voice low and husky.

"Then what is it? Me?"

Yes! she wanted to shout at him. "Look, I'm sure there are plenty of women out there who find you utterly charming. And I'm sure they're all more suited to you than I am."

He gave a disgusted snort. "I hate to wreck this playboy image you have of me, but I rarely date. I sit in a

courtroom or my chambers all day, and at night I'm usually going over cases."

"Then you shouldn't want to waste your time on me."

Harry expelled a frustrated breath. "What I'm trying
to say is that my free time is so precious I don't squander
it. That's why I'd like to spend some of it with you."

Just for a moment Julia felt herself softening toward
him. He wanted to be with her. The idea was wildly flat-
tering. Even though she was still young, it had been years
since she'd thought of herself as a desirable woman, one
that could attract a man.

"You'd better spend that time with someone else. It
would be wasted on me," she repeated, then took a careful sip of coffee. She had to appear natural. She couldn't
let him guess what he was doing to her.

Harry leaned back in his chair and sipped his own coffee. He couldn't understand her rejection. Not just of
him, but of men in general. Maybe he didn't know enough
about women, but there had been moments when she'd
acted as if she liked him. And when they had danced she'd
even rested her cheek on his shoulder. Maybe she was one
of those women who gave mixed signals, he decided. Still,
he was not a man to give up easily.

"Dad used to tell me it does a man good to have his ego
shot to pieces once in a while. Well, you've just shredded
mine."

Julia shook her head helplessly. "It's been nice working for you, Harry. But I can't let things go any further
than that." There. She'd said it as tactfully as she could.
Now the man could leave and get out of her life once and
for all.

He put his cup down and rose to his feet. Julia could
feel his eyes on her, almost as if they were touching her.

"I'm sorry you feel this way, Julia."

She drew in a deep breath, then let it out slowly. "I can't help the way I am."

A mocking little smile curved his lips. "Oh, I think you can. You just don't want to."

Julia was suddenly furious. How dare he say that to her! If it hadn't been for someone like him, her husband would still be alive. Her heart wouldn't be some cold empty thing. She'd still be a wife and Christopher would have a father.

"Please leave. It's getting late." She looked away from him, her jaw rigid with anger.

"I'll leave," he said, "but this is not goodbye, Julia. You might have managed to push other men out of your life, but you're going to discover I'm hard to push."

Julia didn't look around until she heard the door clicking shut. She was shaking all over and she had the strongest urge to run over to the door and shout at him to go and never come back.

Surely he wouldn't have the nerve to show his face again. What kind of man would try to pursue a woman after she'd turned him down flat? Not one, she thought on a more hopeful note. By tomorrow Harris Hargrove would decide she wasn't worth the bother. There was no need for her to worry one more second about him.

Yet Julia did worry. Once in bed, her mind refused to shut down. Every place her thoughts turned, Harris was there. For hours she tossed and turned and tried her best to get him out of her mind. By early morning she stopped trying and gave her pillow a hard whack. She hoped Harry hadn't slept a wink, either.

"Julia, wake up in there!"

Julia heard Rhonda's voice coming from a distance,

then the patter of Christopher's bare feet as he ran by her bedroom door.

"Mommy's still asleep," she could hear Christopher calling from the kitchen. "Want me to go wake her?"

Rhonda laughed. "No, honey. I will. What have you been eating? Peanut butter?"

"I smashed it up with banana. Want some?"

"No thanks, doll. I'll pass on that."

Julia groggily pushed herself to a sitting position as Rhonda breezed into the bedroom.

"Well, well. Aren't we lazy this morning? Did your tête-à-tête with the judge last that long?"

Julia glowered at her friend. "Do you have to be so bright and cheerful this morning?"

Rhonda shrugged and laughed as she plopped down on the bed beside Julia. "Why not? It's a beautiful Monday morning and business is booming. What more could a woman want? Besides a man, that is?" she added.

Julia flung back the covers and swung her legs over the side of the mattress. "Speak for yourself."

Rhonda clucked her tongue. "Oh, Julia. Don't tell me things didn't go well last night with you and Harry. I was all ready to hear something dreamy."

Julia tossed back her disheveled hair. "Ha! If you really want to know, he went away ticked and I was…well, I was upset, too."

Rhonda's brows lifted. "Oh, really? That sounds encouraging. If you managed to make each other mad, there must be some sparks between you."

"You're crazy!"

Rhonda's hand went to her chest in a defensive gesture. "I'm not the crazy one. You are for not latching on to the man."

Julia shook her head as she got to her feet. "I don't want him."

Rhonda fell back against the mattress. "I think you're lying. And I also think you're scared."

Her face grim, Julia reached for her robe. As she wrapped it over her gown she looked at Rhonda. "I am scared, Rhonda. I don't want to fall in love again."

Rhonda shook her head, the amusement gone from her face. "Can you hear yourself? You're twenty-five years old. You want to live the rest of your life alone?"

"I have Christopher," Julia reasoned.

"Christopher will grow up and eventually have his own family. Where is that going to leave you?"

"I have my work and—" She broke off as Rhonda rolled her eyes with sheer frustration. "Look, Rhonda. Harry is not the man for me."

"How do you know? You haven't given him a chance."

"I just know. I want nothing to do with anyone in the legal system."

Rhonda closed her eyes. "Are you going to see him again?"

Julia felt an unexplained sadness wash over her. "I doubt it. I told him in no uncertain terms not to waste his time on me."

Rhonda raised herself back to a sitting position to see Julia seated at her dressing table. She was brushing her long hair with vicious strokes.

"I don't know how you feel, Julia. But I can tell you there are times when I feel so alone. I'd give anything to be wanted and needed. And most of all loved."

Julia stared at her glum reflection in the mirror. There had been many times she'd cried herself to sleep because she missed all those things. "I'm a woman, Rhonda. I feel those things, too. But I loved Carl. How could I, in all good conscience, become interested in a representative of the system that killed him?''

Rhonda got up and took the brush from Julia's hand. "The key word is 'loved,'" she said, brushing Julia's thick mane. "You loved Carl. But that's gone now."

Yes, Carl was gone, Julia thought. Their life together was gone. Still, she couldn't imagine sharing herself with another man. Carl had been the only man she'd ever kissed. She'd married him at nineteen and she'd grown into womanhood not knowing anything about men. All she knew was what Carl had taught her. She didn't know much more about them now.

Julia's heavy thoughts were suddenly interrupted as Christopher bounced into the room.

"I let Auntie Rhonda in," he told his mother while crawling onto her lap. "But she didn't want to eat my breakfast."

Julia kissed the top of his head and hugged him close. "I think Auntie Rhonda would rather eat a proper breakfast. What do you say we go make one?"

"Yeah, like bacon and eggs," Rhonda said with a wink for Christopher.

The child jumped down and latched on to Rhonda's hand. "Come on, Mommy. We're hungry," he said, as the two of them headed out the door.

"I'll be there in a minute," she promised.

Crossing the hall, Julia entered the bathroom. Above the sink, her weary features flashed back at her from the vanity mirror. For long moments she stood there examining the lines and angles of her face, her milky complexion, gray eyes and full lips. She wondered what Harry saw when he looked at her. Did he really think she was attractive?

It didn't matter, she quickly answered. Harris T. Hargrove was a thing of the past.

Chapter Eight

Two days later Julia was playing with Christopher on his gym set. It was late afternoon and the sun was still miserably hot, but she and Rhonda had worked all day in the kitchen. It felt good to be outside spending time with her son, even if the heat was stifling.

"Make me go high, Mommy," Christopher urged as Julia caught the sides of the swing seat. "Then I can be like Josephine."

"Okay, but don't try to flap your wings like Josephine or you'll fall out," she warned him.

Julia gave him a hard push and the swing arced high into the air. Christopher laughed so loudly that Julia didn't hear Rhonda's call until the woman was nearly at her side.

"Julia!"

"What is it?" she asked, finally looking around to see Rhonda waving her arms.

"Mrs. Hargrove's been trying to get you on the telephone. She'd like for you to call her. Here's her phone number." She handed Julia a scrap of paper.

Julia's mouth fell open. "Mrs. Hargrove? You mean Rose? Harry's mother?" Julia asked, completely surprised.

Rhonda nodded. "Yes. I mean her."

"Why on earth does she want to speak to me?"

"I don't know unless it's about doing another party."

"If that was the case she could have given you the details," Julia said.

Christopher was slowing down. He looked over his shoulder at his mother. "Push me again, Mommy!"

"I'll push you, little stinker," Rhonda told him, playfully grabbing him around the waist. She glanced at Julia. "Go call. I'll stay with Chris."

Julia hurried into the house, and as she punched out the numbers, all sorts of questions ran through her mind. Mostly she hoped the woman wasn't calling on her son's behalf. . . .

"Hello. Mrs. Hargrove?" Julia asked when a woman answered.

"Just a moment and I'll call her to the phone."

Julia unconsciously twisted the telephone cord around her finger while she waited. Finally Rose's voice came across the line, and Julia identified herself.

"I'm so glad you returned my call," the woman said. "I was wondering if you might be free later this evening?"

"Er, uh, yes, I believe so," she stammered.

"Splendid. Why don't you and your son come over for supper?"

Julia was stunned, then her mind shot into overdrive. Harry had to be behind this. "I—we couldn't impose."

"Nonsense. My housekeeper is preparing lamb chops and Harry can't make it tonight. They'll go to waste. Besides, I'm really the one who's imposing. I want your barbecue sauce recipe badly."

"Oh, dear. I forgot to give it to Cook. I'm terribly sorry about that."

"It's no problem. Although I would like to try it out this weekend."

Julia pressed a hand to her forehead in an effort to clear her thoughts. If Harry wasn't going to be there, she couldn't see any harm in seeing the woman.

"If you really want us to come, I guess we could make it," Julia told her. "What time should we be there?"

"Six will be fine, Julia. I'll be looking forward to seeing you and meeting Christopher."

Julia made a polite reply and copied down the address Rose gave her. When she hung up the telephone she could hear Rhonda and Christopher in the kitchen.

"Well, what was it?" Rhonda asked when Julia entered the room.

Julia nervously pushed at her tumbled hair. "She wants Chris and I to come over for supper tonight."

"Really? I wonder why I wasn't invited?"

Julia shrugged. "I don't know. See, I promised to give her our barbecue recipe and I forgot to leave it the other night. She wants it for this weekend."

Julia looked at her son. "Chris, go find your new shorts and T-shirt. We're going to have dinner with a nice lady tonight."

Christopher, who was always ready to go anywhere, took off in a run toward his bedroom. "Okay!"

"And find your best pair of tennis shoes under the bed," she called after him.

"So you're going?" Rhonda asked.

Julia started down the hallway to her bedroom. "I didn't see any reason to turn her down. What should I wear?"

Rhonda followed her to the walk-in closet. "Something cool and feminine."

Julia pulled out a pink sleeveless dress with a tight bodice and full gathered skirt. The neck was scooped low in the front and back and edged with tiny white piping. "What about this?"

"You're slim and long-legged. You look beautiful in anything you put on," Rhonda assured her, then plopped down on the dressing bench and asked, "Is Harry going to be there?"

"No!" Julia answered sharply. "That's one of the reasons I decided we'd go. She said he couldn't make it."

"Funny," Rhonda mused aloud, tapping her finger thoughtfully against her chin, "we've never had former clients invite us to dinner before."

Julia suddenly smiled. "You're wrong, dear. Remember Professor Kinard? He invited you out several times."

Rhonda groaned. "Oh, yeah! Along with his white beard and cane."

"He wasn't that old!" Julia giggled at the scowl on Rhonda's face. "And if I remember correctly he had quite a gleam in his eye for you."

"How could you see beyond his inch-thick bifocals?" Rhonda said dryly, then stretched and got to her feet.

Julia began tugging off her tank top. "I'd better go shower."

"Well, I'm going to make myself a big fat fudge sundae and curl up in front of the TV."

With a little wave she strolled out of the room. Julia hurriedly tossed clean lingerie onto the bed along with the pink dress. She gave it one last look before she headed to the bathroom. It didn't really matter what she wore. Mrs. Hargrove only wanted a recipe.

Rose Hargrove lived in a quite area on a pretty cul-de-sac. The house was much more modest than the one Harry lived in, and when Julia rang the bell, Rose answered it herself.

She warmly ushered Julia and Christopher into the house and led them through to a den at the back. "I'm so glad you could make it," she said as they were seated. "I know it was asking a lot of you. Especially when you're so busy."

Julia shook her head. "We finished early today."

Across the room Christopher had discovered two white Persian cats curled up on the back of a leather couch.

"You may pet them, Christopher," Rose told the child. "They love to play." She reached for a rubber ball and a fake mouse filled with catnip on the end table next to her. When she tossed the toys onto the hardwood floor, the sleepy cats suddenly came to life.

Christopher's mouth fell open, then he squealed with delight as the cats began to bat the toys about.

"Christopher fell in love with Harry's dog, Oscar," Julia told Rose. "But I have a feeling he's going to want a cat now."

Rose smiled with affection as she watched Chris and the cats playing on the floor. "Harry's a real animal lover. Like his father was." Her expression grew nostalgic. "They were alike in many ways."

"Well, it's obvious to me that Harry loves you very much."

Rose's smile was a bit regretful. "Yes. But he also misses his father. Their relationship was very close."

Julia's eyes instinctively turned to Christopher. "My husband died shortly after Chris was born."

Rose looked at her with sympathy. "Yes. Harry said you were widowed. It's not something everybody can understand, is it? The loneliness, even the fear we feel at facing the future."

A lump filled Julia's throat. She wished Christopher could have at least known his father as Harry had known his. "No. I suppose no one can until they actually go through it."

Rose suddenly laughed, instantly brightening the moment. "I must say Harry certainly surprised me with the birthday party. Usually my daughter is the one who does things like that. But she married and moved away a few months ago. And she's so busy with her new stepchildren."

Julia asked about the children and for the next few minutes the two women talked about child-rearing. It seemed as though hardly any time had passed when a woman appeared in the doorway to let them know supper was ready.

Over the meal, Julia gave Rose the barbecue recipe, and the exact instructions on how to cook it.

"I love hearty food. So does Harry," Rose said as she put a forkful of lamb in her mouth. "My daughter likes to serve things like pâté and raw vegetables. Which is all right if you like that sort of thing."

Julia was suddenly remembering the day she'd seen Harris in his chambers when he'd been eating the peanut-butter-and-jelly sandwich. She'd been surprised by him. She still was.

"You must be very proud of Harry's being a judge," Julia remarked as she cut into her lamb chop.

"Oh, yes, I am. But to be honest I urged him not to go into the profession."

Julia lifted her gaze to the older woman. "Really? Why not?"

Rose smiled gently. "I don't know if you keep up with law or politics, Julia, but there's such a dirty side to the job. I'm afraid that after a while Harry will become cynical. Right now he's young and he puts his heart into his work."

"Can that be so bad?" she asked, even though she was telling herself that she shouldn't be discussing Harry with this woman. What he did, or didn't do, in his life meant nothing to her. Yet she couldn't seem to deny her curiosity about the man.

"Well, Harry is a man who wants to help anyone who needs it. He'd save the world if he could. Which is noble of him, but that doesn't take away the fact that I'm his mother. I want things for him just like any mother wants for her children. Like a wife, a family."

Julia lifted a bite of food to her lips. "Perhaps your son simply likes being a bachelor."

Rose's expression grew grim. "No, I don't think so. But he prefers it to trying to find a woman who can deal with the demands of his job. I thought he was getting close to marriage once. But it didn't work out."

Obviously it didn't, Julia thought, wondering what the woman had been like.

As if Rose had read Julia's thoughts she said, "Gail was the sort who wanted all of Harry's attention. When he couldn't give it to her they decided to go separate ways. She was a beautiful woman. The last I heard she'd gone out to California to try to get into acting." Rose chuckled. "Which should come easily to her. If you ask me I thought she was acting the whole time Harry dated her."

Julia found herself disliking this Gail. In fact, she didn't like thinking of Harry with any woman but— She quickly quelled the thought.

"Are we going to have brownies for dessert? That's what Harry had," Christopher piped up.

"He did? Well, I don't know what Mildred has made for dessert. But I bet it'll be good," Rose told him, then gave him a wink. "Want to eat it outside in the back-yard?"

Surprised, Christopher looked at his mother. "Can we, Mommy?"

Julia smiled at her son. "That's up to Rose."

"Of course," Rose said. "Sometimes my neighbor comes over to see me at this time of the day. And I do believe he's just about your size, Christopher. I'll bet you two will get on splendidly."

The neighbor, who turned out to be a little redhead named Randy, showed up right after they'd eaten their apple cobbler outside. Christopher was in heaven as the two boys played tag and investigated the small goldfish pond in Rose's backyard. Julia and Rose were content to relax in lawn chairs and enjoy a cup of tea.

"Mother? Where are those lamb chops you were going to have for supper?"

Julia froze. That was Harry's voice coming from the kitchen window.

"We've eaten them all, darling. There's apple cobbler on the bar and tea in the kettle, though."

Julia was trying to think of a good excuse to leave without appearing rude when she heard his footsteps behind them.

"Julia! What are you doing here?"

She turned her head to see him standing just behind her chair. He was holding a bowl of cobbler in one hand and a cup of tea in the other. His face was lined with fatigue as though his day had been a trying one.

Moving to the lawn chair on Julia's right, he took a seat and stretched out his long legs. Through the veil of her lashes, Julia could see he was wearing a pair of dark blue trousers and a white shirt with a pair of blue-and-white striped suspenders. His dark tie was loosened and the top button of his shirt unfastened, revealing dark hair growing at his throat.

"Your mother invited us to dinner," Julia told him, disturbed that the moment she saw him she began thinking how physically appealing he was.

"I'm sorry I couldn't make it. Defense didn't wrap up its case until just half an hour ago."

"It was that murder case about the farm couple, wasn't it?" Rose asked, concern on her face as she eyed her son.

He nodded and dug into the bowl of cobbler.

"Do you think the jury will be out very long?"

His face was grim. "No. They've already reached a verdict. It only took ten minutes."

Julia couldn't help but be interested. "That's rather quick, isn't it?"

He lifted his teacup. "Yes. But it doesn't surprise me. In my time as a judge, I'd never seen such horrendous and damning evidence given in a trial."

"Harry! Harry!"

Christopher came running across the yard, his red-headed friend close on his heels.

"Hello, guys," Harry said, the tiredness on his face disappearing. He looked pointedly at Christopher. "I hear you ate all the lamb chops."

Christopher giggled. "I ate two." He held up two fingers smeared with dirt.

Harry reached out and ruffled his hair. "How's my little partner?"

"I'm good, Harry. Me and Randy been watching the goldfish."

Harry looked pointedly over at his mother. "Don't you think these two guys need a baseball to play with?"

Rose quickly got to her feet. "I should have remembered your old baseball in the storeroom. Come along, boys, and I'll fetch it for you. We might even find a couple of cans of soda in the fridge if we look hard enough."

The boys trotted after her. Just as Chris reached the door, he turned and said, "You won't leave, will you, Harry?"

He shook his head. "I'll be right here. I promise."

Satisfied, Chris followed Randy and Rose into the house. Julia took a deep breath and let it out slowly.

"I didn't know you'd be here," she said quietly. Her fingers nervously pleated the material of her skirt as she fought the urge to look at him.

"I didn't know you'd be here, either," he said. "But I'm glad you are."

She gave him a sidelong glance. The sincere look on his face made her heart turn over.

"Your mother is a lovely woman. It was nice of her to have us for supper."

"Her son is nice, too. If you get to know him," he said with a small grin.

She couldn't help but grin back, but the smile vanished as she remembered all the reasons she shouldn't be interested in this man. "I'm sure he is."

"I can hear a 'but' in there somewhere, Julia." He put his empty dessert bowl on the grass beneath his chair, then rubbed his eyes with the back of his fists. "God, I'm tired."

Julia felt a rush of sympathy. "You should rest more."

"Mmm, that would be nice," he agreed. He dropped his hands and looked at her through bloodshot eyes. "Especially with you."

Color instantly flooded her cheeks. "Harry, I told you—"

"Julia, you might as well face it. I'm not going to give up on you."

Flustered, she got up from the lawn chair and looked down at him. "You don't understand anything about me, Harry. And I—don't want to explain myself. Okay?"

"No. It's not okay."

Turning, she quickly walked across the lawn. She had to put some distance between them before she made a complete fool of herself.

Harry caught up to her at the goldfish pond. When his fingers grasped her upper arm, she tried to twist away.

"Julia, just look at me and tell me what it is about me you don't like. Is it my age? Am I too old for you?"

She turned to face him, and the color in her cheeks deepened to crimson. "No, of course not. I . . . Harry—" She broke off, so confused she didn't know what to say.

"Then maybe you don't like dark-haired men? Maybe you don't like the clothes I wear?"

"Don't be ridiculous!"

His expression became mocking. "You're the one who's being ridiculous, Julia. Don't you know that when a man is turned down by a woman, he wants to know why?"

She turned her face away again, but his fingers still gripped her arm. She was acutely aware of his touch and the fact that he was standing so close to her that her breasts were nearly brushing his chest. "Why are you doing this?" she whispered desperately.

The pleading sound in her voice touched a tender part of him. He didn't want to badger her. Far from it. "Because I think you're running from me—and yourself."

Julia was thankful they were hidden from view by a couple of lilac bushes. "I'm not running—"

Before she could get the rest out, Harry pulled her up against him. She looked up just in time to see his mouth swooping down on hers. The initial shock of it momentarily paralyzed her, but as soon as his warm lips began to move over hers she realized he was kissing her and she wasn't doing a thing to stop it.

Her hands moved up between them and flattened against his chest. But before she managed to lever herself away, his mouth had taken control of hers. She suddenly forgot where they were, or why they were there. His kiss was swamping her, sucking her into a warm, mindless place. God help her, she wanted to hold on to him, taste him, if only for the moment.

"You *are* running, Julia," he whispered against her ear after breaking the contact of their lips.

She drew in a shaky breath. "I suppose the next thing you'll be telling me is that I wanted you to kiss me but I just didn't know it."

To her surprise he laughed softly, causing his chest to move beneath her hands. It made her aware of how close she still was to him and that his hands had moved to her back and were pressing her against him.

"No, I'll tell you that I wanted to kiss you—from the first moment I saw you."

She closed her eyes, wishing she could close out his words just as easily. "This isn't right, Harry," she murmured.

"Just give us a chance, Julia. That's all I'm asking."

Julia could scarcely think when he was so near. He was intoxicating. He wanted her to give them a chance. But deep down Julia knew that if she allowed him into her life she wouldn't have a ghost of a chance of resisting him.

"Mommy! Harry!"

Julia jerked her head in the direction of Christopher's voice. It was probably best her son had interrupted them, she thought with relief. If Harris kissed her again, she might have promised him anything.

"Over here, Chris," she called.

Harry immediately loosened his hold on her and moved a step away, but the look on his face told her that things between them weren't over; they were only just beginning....

Chapter Nine

Two days later, Julia returned from doing a business luncheon for an insurance company to find Christopher's toys strewn all over the living room, and canned spaghetti spilled on the kitchen table, the floor and the cabinets.

"I'm sorry, Mrs. Warren. Things got a little messed up, but I'll have it cleaned up in a flash," the baby-sitter assured her.

Julia waved a hand dismissingly. "Forget it, Michelle. Just clean up the worst of it and I'll get the rest after I change my clothes." She gave Christopher a pointed look. "And we're going to have a little chat, young man."

In the bedroom, Julia shed her slacks and top and pulled on a pair of cutoffs. She'd barely gotten them zipped when the doorbell rang.

"Would you answer that, Michelle," she called. "I'm still dressing."

Julia hurriedly fumbled through a drawer and pulled out a T-shirt with a faded Oklahoma University emblem on the front. She hoped the caller was merely a salesperson she could get rid of quickly. She, and the house, certainly weren't in shape for entertaining friends.

After tugging on the shirt, she hurried down the hall, only to stop dead in her tracks when she reached the living room. Harris was standing just inside the door. Christopher was clinging to one of his legs and Michelle was smiling dreamily up at him.

"He said he was a friend yours, Mrs. Warren, so I let him in."

"That's fine, Michelle. Thank you."

The teenage girl turned back to the kitchen, but not before she'd given Harris one last gooy-eyed glance. Not that Julia could blame her. Dressed in jeans and a navy blue rugby shirt, Harris could have been a rock star or a famous athlete. He certainly didn't look like a judge. But maybe she was thinking that way because deep down she wished he was anything *but* a judge.

"Hello, Harry," she said, walking into the room.

A smile spread across his face and Julia knew he was eyeing her bare legs. She felt practically naked and decided then and there she'd throw the cutoffs in the garbage as soon as he left.

"Christopher tells me you just arrived home. Have you eaten yet?"

"No, I—"

"Good. Would you like to go out for a hamburger?"

"Yeah! Yeah, Mommy! Let's go with Harry!"

Julia cast her son a reproving glance. "And what about the spaghetti you smeared all over the kitchen, young man?"

"I'm sorry, Mommy. I'll help clean it up. I will! I will!"

Before Julia could reprimand him further, the little boy raced into the kitchen. Harry said, "Sounds like Chris has gotten into trouble."

Julia reached up and ran a hand through her tumbled curls. "No more than usual."

He moved a few steps toward her, a sheepish smile on his face. "I guess you're not really thrilled to see me."

What could she say? If she was honest with herself she'd admit that just the thought of him thrilled her, much less seeing him. "You said that—I didn't. Anyway, I'm not going to tell you that you have to leave."

He wiped his hand across his brow in an exaggerated expression of relief. "Whew! I guess I can breathe easy again."

Julia tried to keep from smiling, but found it was impossible to keep the corners of her mouth from tilting upward. She bent down and picked up a miniature road grader and dump truck. Sand poured onto the carpet as she tossed the pair of toys into a nearby cardboard box. "But as far as the hamburger—"

"You'll be happy to go." He walked over to Josephine's cage and peered at the bird. "I take it this is Josephine?"

"Yes, that's the infamous parrot. Watch her—she'll peck you."

"Watch her! Watch her!" Josephine screeched.

"I should take Josephine to court with me. Maybe I could give her some kind of sign when I need to call down an overzealous lawyer. Do you think she could say, 'Objection overruled'?"

Julia laughed. "She can repeat anything if she hears it said enough."

"Believe me, she'd hear it said often enough."

Julia placed the box of toys on the couch, then turned back to him. Her heart was beating faster just knowing he was in the same room with her, but the warm look in his eyes when she caught his gaze made it thump even harder.

"I guess you know you've made Chris very happy. He's been asking about you every day."

"I'd like to think I've made his mother happy, too."

Blushing, she dropped her gaze to the floor. "What do you expect me to say to that?"

He moved closer and placed a finger under her chin, lifting it.

"I don't expect you to say anything. But I'd like for you to say you're glad to see me."

"You're putting me on the spot, Harry. Besides, I don't really know you."

He smiled. "Not yet. That's why I'm here."

A faint smile touched her mouth, but as she looked into his brown eyes the smile grew deeper. She couldn't help but be charmed by him. "Well, I suppose since you've gone to the trouble of driving over here I can't very well say no."

The finger beneath her chin rubbed back and forth, causing tiny little shivers to rush down her spine. For the past two days his kiss had stayed on her mind. Those few moments in his arms she'd come alive in a way she never had before. In fact, she couldn't remember ever losing her head so completely, not even with Carl. As far as fireworks and shooting stars, they'd never occurred when Carl made love to her.

Julia had always believed that kind of passion was only something that happened in fiction. Not in real life.

"You're saying the right thing now," Harry said as if she'd voiced her feelings. His eyes were warm as they held hers.

"I'll have to go change my clothes," she told him, appalled at her breathlessness.

He shook his head. "There's no need for that. You look fine."

Julia glanced down at her T-shirt and shorts. "I can't go anywhere like this!"

Harry grabbed hold of her hand and tugged her toward the door. "Call Christopher," he said. "We're going."

She gave in. Mainly because she knew it would be pointless to argue with him. Every time she tried, she seemed to come up the loser.

In a matter of minutes they were sitting in a fast-food restaurant eating burgers and fries, and drinking thick milk shakes. Apparently there had been a Little League game nearby. The place was swarming with twelve-year-olds in green-and-white uniforms.

"Did you see Josephine?" Christopher asked Harry.

"Yes, I did. She's very pretty."

Christopher crammed a fry into his mouth, chewed and nodded. "She's pretty smart, too."

Amused, Harry glanced at Julia, then back at Christopher. "I'll bet she's not nearly as smart as you are, though."

Giggling, the child shook his head vigorously. "No, 'cause she's just a bird. I'm gonna be a big man someday. Maybe even as big as you. Isn't that right, Mommy?"

"You have to eat to grow as big as Harry," she told him.

Christopher tackled his food with renewed enthusiasm and Harry turned his attention to Julia. "Have you been busy catering?"

She nodded. "Very. What about you? Did you have court today?"

"Yes. A custody trial. I hate them. There's usually one parent who uses the child, or children, to get back at their ex-spouse. It's a sad situation and one that infuriates me."

Julia poked a fry into a glob of ketchup. "You're the judge, though. You have the power to do something about it."

He leaned back in the booth. Christopher was sitting beside him, and he fondly rubbed the top of the boy's head. "Only to a certain point," he replied. "Some of those children are pushed and pulled until they don't know where they belong."

Julia noticed that he talked a lot about children, and she wondered if he'd ever wanted any of his own. He seemed genuinely fond of Christopher, and she instinctively knew he would make a kind, loving father. But that shouldn't sway her feelings toward him.

Suddenly her thoughts came to an abrupt halt. She mustn't have feelings of any kind toward this man!

"Can I go to the playground?" Christopher asked, breaking into his mother's dark musings.

Since they were sitting in a spot where the playground was visible and so she could easily keep a close eye on him, she gave him permission to go.

Once he'd raced outside to the monkey bars, Harry reached across the table to clasp Julia's free hand. Her first instinct was to pull away, but his fingers were warm and strong against hers, and just knowing that he wanted to touch her did strange things to her.

"I've missed you, Julia."

She'd missed him, too. She just didn't want to admit it to him, or to herself. "I can't believe you've been thinking about me."

His thumb rubbed the back of her hand. "Think about you? You've turned my concentration on anything else to mush."

A group of rowdy children passed their table. Yet Julia was hardly aware of their shouting and laughing. She felt as if Harry was leading her into deep, dangerous waters, and she was at a loss as to how to get out.

"I know this isn't the most romantic setting in the world," she heard him saying, "but I didn't think you'd agree to just the two of us at some quiet, dark restaurant."

"I shouldn't have agreed to this," she murmured.

"Why not?"

His hand tightened on hers and her gaze dropped to his mouth. Julia was remembering once again how lost she'd become in his kiss. Would it be that way again?

"Because even if I were in the market for a man, you wouldn't be the right one."

He shook his head. "How can you know that, Julia? You don't really know me yet."

And if she was smart, she wouldn't give him, or herself, the chance to know him better. "I already know... you're not my type."

Harry studied her gray eyes as he tried to figure out what she meant by that. "Well, I might not seem as romantic or attentive as your husband was, but if you'll give me the chance I'll try."

Romantic? Attentive? Carl had never been those things, she realized, and having Harry unconsciously point it out to her, left her feeling guilty and bewildered. Jerking her hand from his, she said with obvious frustration, "I'm not in the market for romance."

"Not in the market for romance, or not in the market for me?" he asked.

His question threw her off guard. *He* threw her off guard. "You won't arrest me if I refuse to answer that, will you?" she asked in an effort to steer their conversation onto lighter ground.

He shook his head, his expression amused. "Judges don't arrest people. That isn't the way the law works."

"I know how the law works!" she blazed. How dare he joke about it?

Harry was taken aback by her furious outburst. He could see from the rapid rise and fall of her breast that she was more than a little disturbed. "My goodness," he said gently, "you certainly prove the old adage that redheads have tempers."

Julia realized she'd almost let him into the private side of her. "I think we should leave. I'll go get Chris."

She fled the booth before he could stop her. He watched her go, wondering just what he'd said that had angered her so much. *I know how the law works,* she'd said, practically spitting every word. Had he somehow managed to find himself attracted to another woman like Gail, who'd resented the time his profession kept him away from her?

Julia was quiet on the drive back to her place. Harry didn't push her to talk. It was his fault that she was angry, he decided. He'd taunted her to a certain point. But he hadn't wanted to make her angry. He'd only wanted her to open up to him. He'd wanted her to share herself, her true feelings. But right now the closed look on her face made his wants seem very remote.

"I hope you won't mind my staying a little longer. I'd like to spend some more time with Christopher," he said when they reached Julia's place.

Julia knew how much Christopher adored Harry. She would be selfish to put her own feelings before her son's. "No, of course not. I have work to do, anyway."

She brushed past him and headed toward the house. If Christopher hadn't been holding on to his hand, Harry would have gone after her and kissed her silly.

"Come on, Chris. Show me the sandpile," he told the boy. "I bet you have some neat toys back there."

The two of them started toward the backyard. Inside the house, Julia went straight to the kitchen to finish cleaning up the spaghetti mess. But once she got there she forgot about the soiled tile and table.

Looking out the window, she could see Christopher sitting in the sandpile with Harry squatting down beside him. With great importance her son was pointing out each miniature piece of his road equipment.

Harry picked up a bulldozer and began to examine it. Their heads came together, Harry's dark and Christopher's tawny. The sight of them so close and so relaxed with each other touched something deep within Julia, and she felt her eyes begin to sting with tears.

If Christopher was old enough to understand his father's death, what would he really think about Harry? Would he hold it against him as she was doing?

The question made her groan aloud. Why did life have to be so difficult? Why did Harry have to seem like such a wonderful man? Why did he have to be a part of the legal system?

Julia pressed her fingers against her closed eyes, realizing as she did that she was shaking all over. Harry was making her look back on her marriage, making her wonder if it had really been as good as she'd believed.

She and Carl had made a child together, but Julia had to admit that Carl had not been a man who'd invited closeness. Nor had he seemed ever to need it from her. He'd always been content with his work, his hobbies and his buddies. Perhaps they hadn't had a deep, sharing relationship.

Damn it, she thought angrily, Harry was making her think too much, feel too much. But the part of her that had been dead and empty for so long was coming back to life. She was feeling things she thought she'd never feel again, and she couldn't deny it felt good.

Harry and Christopher stayed in the backyard for more than an hour. Julia passed the time by tidying the kitchen, then made a pot of coffee and carried a cup through to the living room to where she switched on the TV and settled herself in an armchair.

Darkness had fallen by the time Julia heard the two of them coming through the kitchen. Christopher was chattering nonstop. Harry's deep voice interceded here and there.

As the two entered the living room Julia looked up. Christopher was a grimy but happy mess. Harry looked just as pleased with himself, and it suddenly hit Julia that, try as she might, she could never dislike this man.

"Do I smell coffee?" he asked.

"You do. Have a seat and I'll get you a cup."

He'd expected to find icy anger and was pleasantly surprised at her offer. She left the room and he took a seat on the couch. Christopher climbed up beside him and snuggled against his side.

"I like to watch TV, Harry. Do you?"

He smiled affectionately at the boy. "Sometimes. But I like to read books better."

"What kind of books?"

"All sorts of books with great stories."

"Tell me a story, Harry."

Julia returned with the coffee. He accepted the cup and saucer, then took a careful sip. "Tell you a story. Hmm, let me see," he said thoughtfully. From the corner of his eyes he could see Julia on his left taking a seat. She crossed her long legs and her bare foot began to nervously swipe the air. "Once there was a little girl," he began, "and she had long red pigtails."

"Where did she live?" Christopher wanted to know.

"Oh, she lived on a farm. She had freckles and braces, too, I think. But most importantly she had a pig."

"What was her pig's name?"

"Her name was Ginger, and she was a very pretty pig. The little girl fed her and brushed her and loved her until Ginger was all grown-up. Then the little girl took Ginger to the fair."

"Why did she do that?"

"So that she could enter Ginger in a contest to see who had the prettiest pig in the county."

Christopher giggled. "Pigs aren't pretty!"

"Oh, but this one was. The prettiest pig in all of Kansas, and she won a blue ribbon."

"Then what happened? Did the little girl take Ginger back home?"

"Yes. She took Ginger back home and Ginger became a mother and had a family of little piglets."

"What happened to the little girl?" Chris wanted to know.

Harry glanced at Julia. Her eyes were gentle, almost misty, as they met his.

"The little girl grew up and had a little boy named Christopher."

"That's my name!" He scooted up on his knees and tugged on Harry's arm. "You're joshin' me, Harry."

Harry laughed. "I don't josh little boys like you. Cross my heart."

"Tell me another story!"

Julia spoke up. "No, Chris. You have to get ready for bed now. Go brush your teeth and find your pajamas and I'll be there in a minute to tuck you in."

"Aw, please, Mommy. I want to stay up with Harry," Christopher pleaded.

"Maybe your mother will let me read you a story. Do you have any story books?" Harry asked, remembering how it was when his own mother had sent him off to bed when he would have given anything to stay up.

Christopher nodded at Harry, but his bottom lip began to quiver as he looked at his mother. "Can he read to me, Mommy? Please?"

Julia sighed. "I suppose so. Now go on and do as I told you."

Elated with the small concession, Christopher raced down the hallway to the bathroom. Harry noted the troubled expression on her face.

"Still mad at me?" he asked.

She shook her head resignedly. "I don't know what I am at you, Harry. And if I thought for one minute you were endearing yourself to my son just to get to me I'd boot you out of here."

"But you don't think that," he said with a quiet confidence. "Because you know I'd never do anything so callous. I'd rather chop off my right hand than hurt a child."

No, she knew Harry would never use Christopher. Nor hurt him. In a way that made things even more difficult. If Harry had been selfish and thoughtless, she wouldn't feel drawn to him now.

"Your mother said you came close to getting married once. Why didn't you?"

Her question took him aback. For a moment he merely stared at her.

"Sorry. I shouldn't have asked." She glanced away from him and her foot began to slice the air again.

"I wasn't offended by the question, just surprised," he finally said. "But as for the answer—Gail wasn't right for me. The things we wanted out of life turned out to be entirely different. I wanted children; she didn't. She liked the social life; I didn't. She loved the prestige that went with my position as a judge, but she hated everything else about my job. When I realized that it meant little to her that I was trying to help people, I knew it was time to get out of the relationship."

He was trying to help people, she repeated to herself. Maybe he truly did want to help. Too bad the judge who'd allowed Carl's killer to go free hadn't felt the same way.

"Sounds like she was superficial," Julia said.

"She was," Harris agreed, then drained the last of his coffee before setting the cup on a nearby end table. "But I was much younger and much more impressionable when I met Gail. I've learned a lot since then."

"About women?"

His mouth curved wryly. "About life, my dear Julia."

"I'm ready!"

Both adults turned their heads toward the sound of Christopher's voice. He was dressed in a pair of striped pajamas and standing in the hallway outside his bedroom.

Julia rose to her feet, and Harris followed her to Christopher's bedroom. When she pulled back the sheets printed with tigers and lions, the boy immediately climbed between them, then looked up at Harry with a gamin grin.

"So where are his books, Mother?" Harry asked Julia as he lowered himself into the edge of the bed.

Julia crossed the room to a chest that served as a toy box and pulled out several books. She handed them to Harry, then leaned down and kissed Christopher on the cheek.

"I want your eyes to be closed by the time Harry finishes the story. Okay?"

"Okay," he promised.

She went to the door and looked back at them, then wished she hadn't. She felt guilty and sad at the same time. Christopher's father should be the one reading to him, and it was a man like Harry who had helped take all that away.

Harry glanced through the book. "How about the little boy who lost his shoe? That sounds interesting."

"I like the one about the train that won't quit. 'I think I can, I think I can—'"

"Wait. Don't tell me. Let me read it."

He started the story and Christopher nestled his head back against the pillow. Every now and then he looked up at Harry with adoring eyes. But eventually, as the story neared the end, his eyes fell shut and his breathing deepened.

Harry finished the story, even though he knew the child was asleep. He was a sucker for trains himself. Then he closed the book, reached over and pulled the sheet over Christopher's shoulders.

He was about to switch off the bedside lamp when he noticed the photograph. For a moment he was struck by the sight of a man in a police uniform. Who was this?

Christopher's father? Had Julia's husband been a police-man?

He grabbed the photo and peered at the badge. The name Warren was printed on it, and he knew the district number well. It wasn't far from here. The whole idea knocked Harry off kilter. If Julia's husband had been a policeman and he'd died an early death, it usually meant one thing.

Breathing was difficult as he placed the photograph back down on the table and switched off the lamp.

He found Julia in the living room, sitting in the same chair as earlier. She'd cleaned her face free of what little makeup she'd been wearing and pulled her hair back into a ponytail. She looked very young and, to him, very vul-nerable.

"Chris go to sleep?"

He nodded. "Sound asleep."

"Thank you for reading to him," she said, nervously threading her fingers together as he sat down on the couch.

"It was a pleasure." He patted the seat beside him. "Come here and talk to me."

The huskily spoken invitation made her breath catch in her throat. "I can talk to you here."

"Why are you afraid of me?"

Julia swallowed. "I'm not." She wasn't afraid of him, but rather her strong response to him.

Before she guessed his intentions he leaned over, grasped her hand and pulled her onto the couch beside him.

"Julia, what did you mean earlier when you said you knew about the law?"

Shrugging, she averted her eyes. "Nothing."

"I think you did. And I think it has something to do with the way you've been fighting me."

"You don't know what you're talking about. I haven't been fighting you. It's more like you don't want to take no for an answer."

Harry took hold of her chin and turned her face toward his. "Look at me, Julia. You can't say you didn't feel something when I kissed you."

She glared at him. "What do I have to do to prove to you that I'm not in the market for romance!"

"Kiss me."

Julia gasped. "Kiss you?"

He smiled and brought his forehead against hers. "Yes. You know, put your lips on mine. Your arms around my neck. The rest comes naturally."

"Harry, please—"

"That's all I needed to hear." In one fluid movement he shifted her head against his arm and brought his mouth over hers.

Julia squirmed in outrage, then suddenly stilled as a crazy magic began to sweep over her. The taste, the smell, the feel of him went straight to her senses, and without realizing it she began to kiss him back.

After a moment he pulled slightly away. "There is something between us, Julia. Whether you want there to be or not."

His voice was rough, his lips so close they brushed hers as he spoke. Julia shivered at the sensual contact. "There can't be, Harry. I won't let it."

He lifted his head in order to see her face. "Why, Julia? Because your husband was a policeman?"

Surprise widened her eyes as she stared into his face.

"How do you know that? Did Chris tell you?"

He shook his head. "The photograph by his bed. That's Chris's father, isn't it?"

"Yes."

Chapter Ten

"He was an officer of the law. Like me."

Julia stiffened and pushed against his chest. "No, not like you. You're an officer of the court."

"Law is law. We're all working toward justice."

"I hardly think so!" She stood up abruptly.

Harry followed her as she practically ran to the kitchen. The glow of a street lamp somewhere outside shed just enough light in the darkened room for him to see Julia standing with her back to him by the kitchen sink. He walked up behind her and put his hands on her shoulders.

"Julia," he said softly, "are you trying to tell me that it's not necessarily me, but rather what I stand for that you dislike?"

Spoken aloud by Harry, it sounded so awful, so prejudicial. But she kept remembering Carl lying so still and cold on the hospital gurney. The traumatic sight had changed her life.

"Don't force me to say things you won't want to hear," she whispered hoarsely.

"I think if there's ever going to be anything between us, you have to say them."

His hands were warm on her shoulders and she could feel the heat of his body, not quite touching her, but still so close. She longed to lean back against him, let his strong arms hold her, comfort her.

She took a deep breath. "Carl was a policeman. Here in Oklahoma City. He—" she closed her eyes and gripped the edge of the cabinet counter "—was killed during an armed robbery."

Harry expelled a pent-up breath. "I'm sorry. I know those words are trite. But there's not much to be said—except that one human being killing another is a senseless act."

She twisted around to face him. "Especially senseless when it could have been avoided!"

His eyes roamed her face. The pain was there for him to see. So was the bitterness. He wanted desperately to take it all away.

"You mean he should have never been a policeman?"

"No. I mean Carl's death could have been avoided if a judge had been doing his job!"

There, she'd said it. A weight had been lifted from her shoulders, but sadness was just as quickly dragging her back down. It should be plain to him now that they could never have any kind of relationship.

"A judge," he repeated thoughtfully. "Where did a judge come into all of this? Who was the judge?"

Julia looked away from him as some of the anger drained out of her. "I don't recall his name. All I know is that Carl's killer had been arrested only two weeks before on a robbery charge, but the judge allowed him to go free on bail. If he'd been in jail where he belonged, none of it would have happened!''

How many times had Harris heard that? How many victims had he seen tearing their insides out because the person who had wronged them, or assaulted them, went unpunished? It was something he dealt with every day, but he'd never expected it to hit so close to home.

"I can understand your bitterness, Julia. God knows that our judicial system isn't perfect. But it's the best we have. I know, probably better than anyone, what our policemen are up against."

"Oh, I'm sure. They round them up, you set them free."

He had to fight the urge to shake her. "Don't you think you're being a little bit unfair? You don't know what goes on in my courtroom."

She let out a weary breath and glanced back up at him. "You're right. That is unfair. But I can't help the way I feel." She pulled out of his grasp and moved a few paces away. When he was touching her everything became mixed up inside her. Her heart wanted him, but her mind said no. "So now you can understand—you're wasting your time with me, Harry. But I want you to know that no matter what I've said about law and judges, I...I don't want to hurt you."

Her voice wobbled on the last words, and in that moment Harry knew he loved her. She was a strong, brave woman, perhaps too much so. Everything inside him wanted to show her she needn't shoulder life alone. He wanted to fill her heart with love and happiness.

"You don't have to tell me that, Julia. You don't have the capacity to purposely hurt someone. Not even a judge," he added on a teasing note.

Julia hung her head as tears began to sting her eyes. She tried to blink them away, but they spilled over onto her cheeks, anyway.

"I like you, Harry. I really do," she said honestly. "But that doesn't erase the past."

He moved to her and folded his arms around her waist. Julia resisted at first, but she was too drained and tired to fight him. She rested her cheek against the front of his shirt.

"Nothing will erase the past," he said, his hand lifting to stroke the top of her head. "Right now I'm only asking you to give me a chance, to share your time with me."

It felt so good to be held by him that she could almost believe anything could happen, but Julia knew she couldn't promise something she'd regret come daylight. "I'll share my time with you, Harry. But I can't promise to share more than that."

Three days later Julia found herself in an unfamiliar situation. It was five in the afternoon, there was no work left to do, and she was without her son.

Two hours ago he'd left with his grandparents, who'd driven all the way from Kansas to get him. Julia had been skeptical about letting him visit her parents for a few days. She'd never allowed him to stay away from her overnight, and he'd never been to the farm without her.

But her parents had pleaded and reasoned that both she and Christopher would benefit from the time away from one another. She knew he would enjoy helping his grandfather do chores, and he'd have fun playing with his young cousins who lived close by. The experiences would be good for him, but she was already missing him. The house seemed like a tomb.

She was in her bedroom, deciding whether to drag out the vacuum, when the telephone rang. Taking a seat on the edge of the bed, she lifted the receiver.

"Julia, how are you?"

She recognized Harry's voice immediately and her heart was suddenly racing in her chest. She hadn't heard from him since the night they'd talked about Carl's death. Julia had wondered whether he'd decided it would be best to forget her entirely. Her reaction now to the sound of his voice made her aware of just how much she'd been wanting to hear from him.

"I'm fine, Harry. And you?"

"I've been very busy. I intended to call you yesterday, but I had an arraignment that went on much longer than I'd expected. Are you working this evening?"

She absently twirled the telephone cord around her finger. "No, Rhonda and I finished up about an hour ago."

"Great. I thought—can you come over to my chambers? I'm sitting here alone, waiting for a jury to return a verdict."

Julia's first impulse was to decline, but then she quickly asked herself why she should. Just being with Harry wasn't going to make the sky fall. She could see him without getting serious, couldn't she? And she had promised to spend some of her time with him....

"How long do you expect them to be out?" she asked.

"I honestly don't know. Maybe they'll be back in time for us to take in a late supper. Is it too late to get a sitter for Chris?"

"It so happens Chris has gone to Kansas with my parents."

"Oh. You must be feeling pretty lost then."

"I never knew this house could be so quiet," she said.

"All the more reason you should come over. You remember where my office is?"

"Yes. But..."

"But what? You've decided you don't like me, after all?"

"No. It's just that this sounds like a date."

He laughed softly. "It is, Julia. See you when you get here."

The phone went dead and Julia realized he'd hung up without giving her the chance to turn him down. It was just as well, she thought, because deep down she knew she wanted to be with him.

Thirty minutes later Julia parked near the courthouse and made her way inside. A security guard was pacing the corridor outside Harry's office. She explained to him that Judge Hargrove was expecting her. The guard accompanied her into the outer office, where he knocked on the door.

"Harry, a lady here to see you," he said without ceremony.

The door opened quickly to reveal Harry dressed in robes and wearing his dark-framed glasses. He pulled them off and smiled at the sight of Julia standing behind the security guard.

"Thank you, Jim, for showing Mrs. Warren in."

"Jury back yet?" the guard asked Harry.

"No. Soon maybe." He stood to one side of the door and motioned for Julia to enter.

Jim lingered, shaking his head. "That boy's mother, she was sure upset when the jury went out. She came barreling out into the corridor, threatening to kill you and the DA."

Harry merely smiled. "You've heard talk like that before, Jim. Besides, you know me, I've got a tough hide."

"You'd better have, Harry, if they find that boy guilty." Jim moved off, a troubled look on his face, and Harry shut the door behind him.

"Is that man serious? Was someone really threatening to kill you?"

Harry guided her to a leather couch positioned against one wall. "Just ignore Jim. He's a worrier."

"And you don't worry about things like that?"

He shook his head as he sat down beside her. "If I did, I'd have to get out of the business." Smiling, he took one of her hands between his. "I'm glad you came, Julia. You look beautiful tonight."

Julia had chosen a pair of wide-legged black pants and a black-and-white patterned blouse. The two pieces were made of rayon and moved gently against her body. On the drive over here, she'd had doubts about wearing slacks, but now she was glad she had.

"Thank you. I hope I've dressed appropriately. You didn't say where we'd be eating."

"I'll let you decide," he said, his face happy as he relaxed against the cushions.

It was obvious he was glad to see her. Julia's spirits soared in spite of her intentions not to let herself be affected by him. But his smile was too warm to resist, and the feel of his hands cocooning hers made her feel wanted and special.

She smiled back at him, feeling a bit like a high school girl out on her first date. "That might be dangerous," she said playfully.

"I'll take my chances," he told her, his brown eyes gleaming as they moved over her face. "So tell me how your parents ever managed to get Chris away from you. I'm sure it wasn't easy."

She laughed. "Am I really that much of a mother hen?"

"No. I just happen to know how much you love him." It was one of the first things he'd admired about her.

"Well, I realized, it would be good for him to be on the farm for a few days. He'll come back sunburned and a pound heavier from Mom's homebaked cookies."

"Mmm. Sounds nice. I wouldn't mind going myself."

She laughed softly and her eyes twinkled. "I can't imagine you on a farm, Harry."

He feigned a hurt look. "You can't judge a judge by his looks. Even though I told you I don't know much about agriculture, I have been on a farm. I've even hauled hay."

"You're kidding!"

He laughed at her shocked expression. "No. I had a friend in college who lived on a farm in Illinois. I stayed a month with him between classes one summer. It was a time I'll never forget."

"It made a man of you, no doubt," she said.

"No, it made me realize I was more cut out to be a lawyer than a farmer."

Julia laughed. "How so?"

"I enjoyed giving the cows a closing argument more than giving them their hay."

"You're teasing me now."

He shook his head. "No, I really did give them a closing argument. But you have to remember I was only twenty at the time and was already seeing myself as a member of the supreme court."

The smile on Julia's face faded. "Would you still like to go that high in your profession?"

"No," he said quickly. "Even if I could, I wouldn't. There's too much of a need for judges on the local level. And I want to be where I'm needed the most." He got to his feet. "Would you like coffee or a soft drink while we're waiting?"

Before Julia could answer, a light rap sounded on a door just down the wall from where she sat. Since it wasn't the door she'd come in, she figured this one must lead into the courtroom.

"Excuse me, Julia," he said and went to open the door.

It was the bailiff. "The jury is back, Your Honor," he said to Harry.

"I'll be right there, Dale." He shut the door and turned back to Julia, while tightening the knot in his tie. "Julia, if you like, you can go around to the public seating in the courtroom. You might find it interesting to hear the verdict."

She rose to her feet. "Yes, I will. What's this trial about?"

With a frown and a shake of his head as he reached for his glasses, he replied, "What a big part of them are about these days—drugs. Specifically marijuana. Oklahoma has a wonderful climate for it, you know."

She wondered if he meant the weather or the economy. Both, she imagined.

Harry went out the door and she could hear the bailiff instructing all those present in the courtroom to rise. By the time she made it to the courtroom everyone was already seated again and Harry was accepting the verdict from the bailiff.

She slipped quietly onto a wooden bench in the back of the room and glanced around. There were very few people in the room other than the lawyers and the defendant, a young man with lanky blond hair and a pitted complexion. Behind the defendant's table, in the public seating, was a handful of people, but Julia was directly behind them and couldn't see their faces.

Harry soberly read the guilty verdict and instructed the accused that he would be sentenced two weeks from today in this same courtroom.

He'd barely gotten the words out when a woman in the group jumped to her feet and cried, "My boy is innocent!" She jabbed an accusing finger in Judge Harris's direction. "This ain't over, judge! He ain't going to jail!"

Harry slammed down his gavel. "Bailiff, will you please remove this person from the courtroom before I fine her with contempt?"

The bailiff quickly grabbed the small, dark-haired woman by the arm and forcibly escorted her down the aisle to the back of the room. As they passed Julia, she caught a glimpse of the woman's face. She'd never seen such a venomous expression on anyone, and the thought that this much hatred was directed at Harry shook her deeply.

She sat there quietly for a few minutes, her head bowed, almost unaware that everyone else had left the courtroom. Then Harry's deep voice interrupted her musings.

"Julia, let me get a few things from my office and change out of my robes. I'll only be a minute."

She looked up to see that Harry had stepped down from the bench and come down the aisle to her side. "I'll wait here for you," she told him.

He disappeared into his chambers and Julia looked thoughtfully around the courtroom.

It was an authoritative room. One where, no doubt, serious decisions were made every day concerning people's lives. Her life had been changed forever in a room such as this. If one man had made a different decision four years ago, Carl would perhaps be alive today.

But that man wasn't Harry, Julia tried to reason with herself. All judges weren't the same. A judge couldn't be judged by his looks, as Harry had said. Maybe they could be judged on their work in the courtroom. Maybe if she saw him doing his job, she could understand the judicial system better. Then perhaps she could understand why it had been instrumental in the death of her husband.

A few minutes later Harry and Julia walked down the steps of the courthouse and headed toward the parking lot. It had grown dark, but the temperature was still in the high nineties. A southerly breeze was rattling the leaves of the trees and teasing the auburn hair lying loose on Julia's shoulders.

"Did the guilty verdict surprise you?" she asked Harry as he unlocked the passenger door of his white BMW.

"No. The state had plenty of evidence against him."

Julia slid inside and waited for him to go around and take his place behind the steering wheel.

"Then why was his mother shouting he was innocent?" she asked as he started the engine.

Harry's expression was wry as he glanced at her. "Wouldn't you want to believe Chris was innocent?"

Julia thought about that remark while he maneuvered the car onto the street.

"Of course. But if he was guilty—" she looked at him "—I would have to accept the fact, even though it hurt. Why didn't you fine her for her outburst?"

"I could have," he said. "But I believe sending her son to prison will be enough punishment. Besides, I really doubt she could have paid the fine. Then she would have been forced to do time in jail. Which means the county would have had the expense of housing and feeding her."

He shrugged as though the endless circle of the law was something he'd long ago learned to live with. "Our jails are already overflowing, and we need the space for more violent lawbreakers."

Julia looked at him in disbelief. "And she wasn't violent? My Lord, the security guard said she was threatening to kill you!"

He chuckled softly. "It's nice to have you concerned about my safety, Julia. But I can assure you the woman is harmless on that score. It's the quiet ones you have to watch."

Julia started to ask him if he'd had any bad experiences with the "quiet ones," but then stopped herself. She was getting too personal, too familiar with him. She shouldn't want to know what went on in his life.

"Where would you like to eat?" he asked, breaking into her thoughts.

"Is there any kind of food you don't like?"

"Do I look like a finicky eater? I'll eat anything that doesn't get up and crawl off the plate."

She shuddered and made a face at him. Harry laughed. "You don't cater anything like that, do you?"

"No! And you wouldn't have hired me if I had."

His features suddenly softened. "I'm very glad I did hire you. Otherwise we might never have met."

He pulled his eyes off the traffic to glance at her, and Julia shrugged awkwardly. "I don't know why. I haven't been very nice to you."

He laughed again. "You have. In your own way. But sometimes it's hard to believe you were married. Was your husband the only man you'd ever dated?"

She was both irritated and surprised by his question. "Yes. But how did you know?"

"You don't seem very comfortable around men. Or maybe it's just me?"

"I'm learning to relax around you," she admitted.

His brows lifted wryly. "Really? Are you relaxed now?"

"Sort of."

Before she realized his intentions he reached for her hand and pulled her closer to him.

"Now you are, aren't you?" he asked, a teasing gleam in his eye.

Julia should have scolded him. Instead, all she could manage to do was laugh. "You're a crazy man."

He let out a contented sigh and curled his fingers around hers. "And it feels good. Do you know how nice it is to have you here with me after a day in court?"

Julia shook her head. "No. But I was just thinking that maybe I should watch a few of your cases."

"Why?" He was surprised. She'd seemed so against the system when they'd talked of her late husband.

She looked down at his hand curled around hers. It felt so good to be touching him, she had to admit. She was tired of lying to herself, pretending that he meant nothing to her. He did, God help her.

"The legal system is so complicated. Maybe **it** would help me understand it better."

His fingers tightened around hers. "You don't have to understand the law to understand me, Julia," he said gently.

Her face grew sad. "I suppose I've been narrow-minded about Carl's death. I try to tell myself I have been. And Rhonda's always telling me I should put it in the past. But telling myself and doing it are entirely different things."

Harry wished she could put it in the past, too. He wanted to be the man in her thoughts instead of her dead husband's ghost.

Chapter Eleven

Julia had chosen a seafood place. When they got there the place was crowded, but the hostess managed to find them a table in a corner away from most of the noise.

Harry ordered wine and after the waiter had poured some in each of their glasses, Julia took a sip and glanced out over the sea of linen-covered tables. Several of the nearby diners were casting glances their way and Julia wondered if they recognized Harry.

"I think those people know you," she said.

He looked in the direction of her gaze. "Maybe. But I don't know them. I meet so many people, especially when I'm campaigning."

Julia looked at him curiously. She'd forgotten that his was an elected position. "That's right, you have to campaign. Do you like that part of it?"

He shook his head. "I don't like to push myself on people."

Julia burst out laughing. She couldn't help herself. "You? Don't like to push yourself on anyone? I think I could disagree with that."

His grin was sheepish. "Well, other than you, Julia. But you forced me to do that."

She looked at him over the rim of her wineglass. "I can't understand you, Harry. I'm nothing like you. I don't know why you want to spend time with me."

He reached for her hand and she blushed as he lifted her fingers to his lips. "I don't understand why you underestimate yourself. You're a beautiful woman, Julia. Any normal, red-blooded man would want to spend time with you."

Julia had never thought of herself as beautiful. She'd never tried to be beautiful. But to hear Harry say she was lifted her heart.

A waitress arrived and he released her hand. Julia busied herself spreading the linen napkin across her lap and missed the light in Harry's eyes as he watched her.

With each moment he spent with Julia, he felt himself falling more deeply in love with her. She was a soft, gentle woman at heart, in spite of her intentions to cling to the bitter past. And knowing that made him even more determined to win her love.

After a delicious dinner, they drove back to the courthouse to pick up Julia's car. From there Harry insisted on following her home to make sure she got there safely.

Julia figured he was using the excuse to spend more time with her. But she wasn't going to make a fuss about it. She kept telling herself, spending time with Harry didn't mean she had to get serious about him.

"Would you like to come in for coffee?" she asked after he'd parked behind her and climbed out of his car.

"Why Julia, you're actually softening," he teased, taking her by the hand as they walked toward the dark house.

"I'm not softening," she denied. "I'm merely being gracious."

"For buying you a wonderful dinner," he said teasingly.

"Of course. It's nice not to eat my own cooking once in a while." She fished the house keys out of her purse and handed them to Harry.

He opened the door and Julia reached in and flipped on the light. Josephine immediately began to screech.

"Hush, naughty bird!" Julia scolded lightly. She tossed her purse onto an end table, then turned back to Harry. "If you don't mind, I'd like to call my parents to make sure they got home safely."

"Sure, go ahead," he said. "I'll talk to Josephine."

He went over to the bird cage and poked his finger between the wires. The bird hopped on its pedestal and ruffled its feathers. "Chris! Chris!"

"You have it all wrong, bird. My name is Harry. See if you can say that. Harry," he repeated patiently. "Har-ry."

Julia's expression was amused as she punched out the numbers of her parents' phone. "She only says the name of people she likes. To this day she's never said Rhonda," Julia told him while waiting for the call to go through.

"Well, Josephine, you're going to like me, aren't you?" he crooned to the bird.

Behind him, Julia's conversation was short. After she hung up, she came over to where he was still unsuccessfully coaxing the parrot. The scent of her perfume swirled around him, reminding him how close she was and that the two of them were completely alone. "How are things at your parents'?" he asked.

"Fine. Mom said Chris was already in bed fast asleep."

"I'll bet you're missing him far more than he's missing you."

Julia's quiet laugh was rueful. "I'm certain of that."

Her eyes lifted to his face and for long moments they just stood and looked at each other.

"I go home to an empty house every night," he said softly. "I always thought I liked it that way. But now I'm not so sure."

Julia's breathing was suddenly shallow. "You... wouldn't say that if you knew what it was like living with a four-year-old boy."

His hand reached up and touched the auburn halo of her hair. "Little boys eventually go to sleep."

How long had it been, she wondered, since a man had looked at her the way Harry was looking at her? Had a man ever really looked at her that way? Erotic, dangerous thoughts were running through her head. Things she shouldn't be thinking at all. But with Harry so close, it seemed as natural as breathing.

"Harry, I..."

His hand moved down until it was cupping the side of her face. "You're so beautiful, Julia. I've thought so from the moment I first saw you."

Her breath drew in sharply as she felt her resistance slipping. "The coffee... I'd better..."

"I don't want coffee," he whispered with a shake of his head. "I want you."

The word *no* was on her tongue, but it never made it past her lips. He was drawing her into his arms, pressing his mouth down on hers.

A tiny groan of surrender sounded in Julia's throat as she gave in to the kiss. His arms tightened, enfolding her into the cocoon of his embrace.

There was a sweet mystery in the way his lips explored hers, and Julia responded instinctively. Through the thin material of her blouse, she could feel his hands on her back, leaving trails of fire wherever they touched.

Eventually they moved to her face again to hold it fast while he kissed her hungrily. Julia was vaguely aware of the texture of his fingers, the scent of his skin, the scrape of whiskers as he moved his face against hers.

"Julia," he breathed, breaking their kiss, "do you know what you do to me?"

She knew much more about what he did to her. He made her crazy. He made all her common sense fly out the window. "I didn't mean to kiss you like that," she said huskily.

"You didn't?"

There was amusement lacing his voice. Julia shuddered and goose bumps dotted her skin as he began to nuzzle her cheek and ear.

"No. I kissed you like a lover—and that was a mistake. Because...we aren't lovers," she finally managed.

"We could be. If you'd only trust me," he whispered.

She shook her head, but he ignored the gesture. His mouth moved against her throat, his hands slid to her breast. Julia let out a small moan of protest but it was the only resistance she could muster. He was making her come alive with all sorts of delicious feelings.

"Harry, this is wrong. I'm not the woman you think I am," she said in a voice throttled with desire.

Laughter gurgled in his throat, and before she knew what he was doing, he lifted her in his arms and carried her to the couch.

"I know the woman you are, Julia," he said, taking a seat with her still cradled in his arms. "You're the one who doesn't know yourself. Right now, you're trying to tell yourself you don't want me. But you do. I can feel it every time I touch you.''

"Maybe I do," she whispered reluctantly. "But that doesn't make it right.''

"Because I'm a judge," he said grimly. "Is that what you think about when I kiss you?''

Julia tried to sort out her confused thoughts. What *was* she thinking? She was thinking she wanted him to go on kissing her forever, that she wanted him to make love to her. And that was where the *wrong* came in. She *should* be remembering he was a judge. Because in the sobering light of day she was sure to remember that he belonged to a profession that had helped to kill her husband. To love him would make her a traitor to Carl and their marriage. She couldn't live with that!

"Harry, I just don't want to do this," she pleaded.

"Oh, Julia, why do you keep fighting it?''

"Fighting it?" she echoed, her gray eyes wide as she looked up into his face. "Because I—''

Her answer was smothered by his mouth staking claim to hers. Julia felt everything inside her turning to hot putty as his lips asked her to respond to him.

She felt him shifting her weight onto the couch and then he was next to her, his hard chest pressed against her soft breasts. Somewhere along the way she gave up fighting the desire she felt for him. Her arms pressed around his neck, and her mouth opened beneath the probe of his tongue.

His fingers fumbled with the buttons on her blouse and then he was pushing the thin fabric away. Her skin was hot against his hands, and when he removed the scrappy lace from her breasts, her nipples hardened into waiting rosebuds.

"Julia, you're so beautiful," he choked out, lowering his head. She actually cried out with pleasure as his moist mouth drew in the peak of one breast. She'd never intended to let him go so far, but her body was betraying her. It wanted him so desperately. The ache that had started in the lower region of her body was beginning to consume her.

It had been so long since she'd had a man holding her like this, so long since she'd felt the need to give herself and take back what she needed. Not since— Her body's building desire skidded to an abrupt halt and she stiffened beneath him.

Harry must have been aware of the sudden change in her because he lifted his head. His face was puckered with confusion. "Julia?"

"I can't do this, Harry. I can't."

Slowly he eased away from her and Julia sat upright and pulled her blouse over her bared breasts. Harry could see the distress on her face and wished he knew what put it there. He'd been so lost in her that all he'd been able to think about was making love to her. "Julia, I'm sorry if I hurt you."

She watched him rake his fingers through his black hair. There was a tremor to his movement that matched the one inside her. Suddenly she felt very guilty and very helpless.

"It's not you, Harry. It's me. The problem is with me."

He let out a heavy breath and turned to see a tear glistening on her cheek. "I'm sorry, Julia. I know you're not ready for this, or me. And every time I'm away from you I promise myself I'm going to go slow. That I'm going to give you time to come to terms with me—and with the way your husband was killed. But when I'm near you—" he reached for her hand and slid his fingers intimately between hers "—I just want to make love to you."

Julia hung her head, then swung it back and forth. "I can't make this guilt inside me go away, Harry. I want it to, but I can't."

His expression was grim as he studied her. "Why should you feel guilty? You're a woman with flesh-and-blood needs and desires. There's nothing wrong with letting yourself love another man."

Love. Is that what he wanted? Her love?

"Julia, it's not your fault that your husband was killed. Are you supposed to forfeit happiness because his life was taken?"

She looked at him, her eyes pleading. "Don't you understand that I feel like a traitor? Carl loved me and—"

"And you loved him. I understand that's something you haven't forgotten."

Everything went still inside Julia as his words echoed through her. She twisted away from his gaze.

"No, you don't. Because I didn't understand myself until a few seconds ago," she whispered hoarsely.

The broken sound in her voice caused pain to fill Harry's chest. "Julia—"

She lifted her face back up to him. "I didn't love Carl. Not really," she said bleakly. "I thought I did, but . . ."

Harry couldn't bear to see her torturing herself. Closing the space between them, he took her gently by the shoulders. "Why are you doing this to yourself, Julia? I'm sure you were a good wife to Carl."

Shaking her head, she let out a deep sigh. "I thought I was, but he deserved more than just a wife who was good to him. He deserved my love. When I look into my heart now . . . I know I didn't give him that part of myself."

Harry could see the agony on her face, but he was at a loss as to how to make it go away. While moving his fingers in a soothing motion against her shoulders, he spoke softly. "Julia, sometimes two people grow up together and become very close and comfortable with each other. If that's what you and Carl had together, then there's nothing wrong with that. You can't make yourself love someone. That isn't the way it works."

"So that means it's all right for me to go to bed with a judge?" she asked bitterly.

Harry felt like shaking her. "I haven't asked you to go to bed with me," he said sharply. "But would it be so awful if I did? I'm human, Julia. If you'd start thinking of me as a man with human needs instead of a judge on a bench, then maybe you'd see things as they really are!"

At the moment Julia was so fraught with guilt and confusion she couldn't see anything. "I think . . . you'd better leave," she said jerkily.

Harry dropped his hands defeatedly from her shoulders. "Sure you want me to leave. So you won't have to deal with me or the things I make you feel." He started toward the door, then looked back over his shoulder at her. "Go ahead and hold it against me because of who I am, or what I am. I've dealt with prejudice before."

Julia felt as if he had slapped her. For long moments after he'd gone out the door she stood motionless, pain squeezing like a clenched fist in her breast. Impossible questions seemed to be tearing her thoughts first one way, then the other. She loved Harry, but she didn't know if she'd ever be able to forget who or what he was.

"Harry! Harry! Harry!"

Julia turned at the sound of Josephine's sudden squawking. "Hush up, Josephine! He's gone. He can't hear you now."

Julia slept badly and it showed on her face when she met Rhonda in the work kitchen the next morning.

"Goodness, Julia, I know you didn't want Chris to go to Kansas, but that's nothing to cry about."

Julia darted a swift glance at her friend as she gathered the makings for coffee. "Who said I've been crying?"

"Your puffy, red-rimmed eyes, that's who," Rhonda said knowingly. She put her arm around Julia's shoulder. "Honey, Chris is going to have a wonderful time. Your parents won't let anything happen to him."

Julia's gaze dropped guiltily away from her friend. "I'm not worried or upset about Chris. I miss him, but that's all."

Rhonda's face puckered with concern. "Well, something has gotten you upset. What is it?"

Julia made a frustrated sound. "Oh, I had a round with Harry last night."

"Harry?"

Julia moved to the cabinet counter and began to spoon coffee grounds into a drip basket. "Yes, you know. Judge Harris T. Hargrove," she said dryly.

As they waited for the coffee to brew, Julia related some of what had happened between her and Harry.

"Oh, Rhonda, I've never been so confused. I use to think my life was very simple, that it would continue to be simple. But Harry..." Sighing miserably, she sank into a chair, then said, "Oh, I feel so guilty. He's filled my head with all sorts of questions about myself. He stirs me up in ways that Carl never did."

Rhonda studied her carefully. "You mean physically?"

Julia's face flamed. "Yes."

Rhonda made an impatient gesture. "For Pete's sake, that's nothing to feel guilty about."

"No, maybe not. But sometimes..."

"Sometimes what?" Rhonda prodded, seeing the pain on Julia's face.

"Sometimes," Julia whispered, "I'm afraid Harry is right. I didn't love Carl wildly or romantically. I just sort of fell into a relationship with him."

Rhonda gave her a wry, knowing look. "And now that Carl is gone you feel guilty about that, because you think he deserved better?"

Julia nodded.

Rhonda sighed. "My dear friend, you were a good wife to Carl. I was a friend to you both. I should know. Carl didn't want or expect more from you."

Julia reached for her coffee. "He should have."

"You should have expected more from him, too. But that's all in the past. That shouldn't affect you and Harry now. Why are you punishing him?"

Julia sipped her coffee as she thought about her friend's question. Is that what she was doing to Harry? Punishing him?

"I don't want to punish him. I just don't know if I can deal with what he does, who he is. I'm afraid if I let things go any further, one or both of us is going to get terribly hurt."

Rhonda frowned. "From the looks of your red eyes, I think it's already gone that far."

That afternoon Julia was putting the finishing touches on a wedding cake when someone knocked on the door.

Rhonda went to answer it. When she opened the door on a huge bouquet of white roses she let out a squeal of delight.

"Are those for me?" she gasped.

A delivery boy peeked out from behind the greenery. "Are you Julia Warren?"

Rhonda groaned with disappointment. "No. But she's here." Rhonda plucked the bouquet from him and dropped a tip in his hand. "Thanks. I'll give them to her."

By now Julia had put the tube of frosting aside and was looking curiously across the room at Rhonda and the roses in her arms.

"Hmm. Looks like you made a hit last night with your businessman," Julia teased.

Rhonda laughed. "He was about as romantic as a flea on a hound's back." She hurried over to Julia. "Hurry, open the card."

Julia's mouth dropped open. "They're for me?"

Rhonda nodded, a knowing look on her face. "And I'll bet we both know who they came from."

Julia grimaced. "Probably my mother. My sister's birthday is tomorrow and she often gets it confused with mine." Julia found the small envelope and pulled out the plain white card. The message was brief, but went straight to her heart: *Forgive me. Harry.*

Rhonda smiled and handed the bouquet to Julia. "Does this mean you're going to see him again?"

Julia's eyes lingered on the roses. Their pristine white petals were a subtle reminder that there were still unsullied things left in the world. Maybe Harry was trying to tell her that. "He may not want to see me again. I said some awful things to him."

Rhonda let out a disbelieving laugh. "Girl, do you think the man would waste his time and money sending you roses if he didn't want to see you again? You have a lot to learn about men."

No, she had a lot to learn about Harry, she thought. But would that be wise? she asked herself. Would she come away with an ache in her heart far worse than the one she had now?

* * *

It was almost eight o'clock by the time Julia backed her car out of the driveway and headed toward Harry's. Going to see him might not be the right thing to do, but after agonizing over it all day, she'd made a decision and she wasn't going to turn back now. For the past four years she'd been turning back, looking back, thinking back. If she was ever going to get out of the past, she had to move forward, somehow, someway.

Julia's confidence waned, however, when she pulled her car to a stop in front of his house. She got out slowly and wiped her damp palms against her jeans. She'd dressed casually so as not to let him think she'd gone to any trouble to impress him. But she'd carefully twisted her unruly hair into a French braid and applied a little mascara and lipstick.

She punched the doorbell and waited. In moments he answered the door. He was wearing only a pair of old jeans, his feet and chest bare.

Julia was so taken in by the sight of him she almost missed the utter surprise on his face.

"Julia!"

Her lips trembled as she forced them into a smile. "Er, am I interrupting anything?"

Shaking his head, he swung the door wide. "Not at all. Come in."

Julia stepped through. As he shut the door he fought the urge to pull her into his arms. He wanted to know why she was here and he couldn't risk the chance of angering her before he found out.

"Let's go to the den," he said. "It's more comfortable there."

Julia allowed him to lead her through the dark house. As they entered the den, she could hear muted music, then her eyes caught sight of several papers scattered across a low coffee table. To one side was a tray with a teapot and an empty cup.

"I've interrupted your work," she said.

He dropped his hand from her arm, but didn't move away from her. Julia forced herself to look up and into his eyes.

"Don't you know you're more important to me?"

Julia's heart began to race. "I came to tell you that I'm sorry about my..." Shaking her head, she started again. "I overreacted and..."

"Oh, Julia," he said gently, "there's no need to say anything to me. Just the fact that you're here makes me happy."

It made her happy, too. Far more than it should have. "Thank you for the roses, Harry. But I would have forgiven you, anyway," she said, a wry smile on her lips.

He grinned down at her. "That's nice to know. You were really angry with me last night."

Her brows lifted, then fell. "You were really angry, too."

He reached out and touched her shoulder, caressing it gently. Julia wanted to melt into him.

"We do rub sparks off each other," he said, then guided her toward a chintz couch. "Would you like a cup of tea?"

Julia shook her head. "No, thanks. Rhonda and I worked a wedding reception this evening and I'm still full of leftovers."

He gathered up the scattered legal papers and stacked them on the end of the coffee table before he joined her on the couch.

When he settled back against the cushions and looked at Julia, a hundred questions bombarded him, but he couldn't find it in him to voice even one. He didn't want to move too fast and break this fragile truce between them.

Julia's gaze dropped to her folded hands. "I felt badly after you left last night."

"I felt badly, too."

Julia let out a pent-up breath. "You forced me to think about things that, frankly, I didn't want to think about."

He shook his head ruefully. "Julia, I was out of line, but—" he moved closer and took her hand in his "—I'm selfish where you're concerned. I want to be the man in your thoughts. The only one."

She didn't say anything. She couldn't admit to him just how much he'd been consuming her thoughts.

"Last night," he went on, "when I implied you didn't love your husband—I wasn't trying to take anything away from the relationship you had with him. I only wanted you to see things as . . . I see them."

Sighing, she lifted her head. "I'd always believed Carl and I had a good marriage. And we did, in some aspects. But whether I was truly in love with him . . ." She shook her head sadly. "I just don't know anymore. I cared for him and respected him. If that's love, then he had that much from me."

Harry wanted that from her, too. But he also wanted more. He wanted her to be blindly, passionately, in love with him. The kind of hot, sweet love that never cooled or faded away.

"It wasn't your fault that he was killed. Nor was it mine," he said simply.

Somewhere inside Julia, a part of her knew that. But there was always that other part that wouldn't let the grief and bitterness go. "Don't you think I tell myself that?" she asked desperately.

Shifting closer to him, she lifted her hand and cupped the side of his face with her palm. "When I look at you, Harry, I don't want to see you as a judge. I don't want to know that you're a part of the legal system."

His fingers tightened on her hand. "But I am part of it, Julia. I can't change that. I don't want to change that."

"I don't want you to change, Harry," she said quietly. "I really don't." She wanted to change herself. But she just didn't know how, or if she could.

"Julia, the other night you talked about coming to court. Maybe if you did..."

"Would you really like for me to?" she asked.

Harry studied the sweet, young lines of her face. No, truthfully, he didn't want her in his courtroom. He didn't want her exposed to the dirty, sickening crimes he dealt with. There were times even he found them hard to listen to, and times he carried some of the testimony of the victims around in his head for days because it was so horrifically real he couldn't forget it.

No, he didn't want Julia to have the same experience. But he didn't know any other way to show her that he was just like any other man trying to do his job. Just because he was a judge didn't mean he was God. He didn't have the power to stop robberies or assaults or murder, or the pain those things caused others. She had to see and understand that or she would never be able to love him fully.

"I told you last night that to understand me you didn't have to understand the law. But maybe I was wrong about that. You don't seem to be able to separate me from the law, or the law from me."

That was true enough, Julia thought dismally. She also couldn't forget how it felt to be in his arms. At this moment she wished she could put everything aside and ask him to make love to her. "Harry, since Carl's death, I told myself I didn't need or want a relationship with another man. It's hard for me to convince myself I want one now. Much less a relationship with a judge.''

"I'm a man for God's sake, Julia! Just remember that when you sit in the courtroom." He drew her close and cradled her face in his hands. "You'll give me that much, won't you?"

Julia felt herself trembling as desire shot through her. "I want to give you much more, Harry. I'm just afraid to."

With an anguished groan he pulled her head against his shoulder and pressed his face in her hair. "Don't be afraid, Julia. We'll take things one step at a time."

Chapter Twelve

The next morning Julia rushed to get her work finished so she could drive to the courthouse. Harry had said a mail-fraud case was being tried today and she wanted the chance to see him work.

After their talk last night, Julia felt better than she had in days, in years even. She knew she loved Harry. It was not a question in her mind anymore; it was a certainty. And if she gave herself time, she really believed she could get past the fact that he was a judge.

However, her plans to go to court were cut short, when she was surprised with the arrival of Christopher and her parents.

Harry whistled as he walked down the corridor to his courthouse office.

"You sound awfully happy, Judge. Does that whistling have anything to do with that pretty redhead who came to see you the other day?"

Harry glanced over his shoulder at Jim, the security guard.

"It just might be," he said with a grin.

"Hmm. Well, this sounds serious."

"It just might be," Harris said again.

Jim chuckled. "She must be something special. I can't remember the last time I saw you with a woman."

"Well, for a long time I've been gun-shy. But Mrs. Warren came along and knocked me off my feet."

"Mrs. Warren," the guard repeated. "She's been married?"

After working with Jim for six years, Harry had grown used to the man's personal questions. "Yes. She's a widow. Her husband was a policeman killed in the line of duty."

"Oh, that's too bad. Warren, did you say? That name sounds familiar."

"Carl Warren. It happened during an armed robbery about four years ago."

For a moment Jim plied his memory, then suddenly he snapped his fingers. "Yeah. I remember now. He was a young officer. And the guy that shot him got put on death row. Guiddard his name was, wasn't it?"

Harry nodded, then excused himself as he entered his offices. Edith was already behind her desk, typing. She looked up at him over the rims of her glasses.

"Morning, Judge. You've got a busy day ahead of you."

His mind was churning so he didn't even register her comment. Absently rubbing his forehead, he said, "Edith, I want you to find something for me. Pull up anything you can find on a Guiddard case. And can you do it right away?"

"I'll have it on your desk before you finish your morning coffee," she assured him.

Half an hour later, Harry wished Edith hadn't been quite so efficient. In fact, he wished Jim had never brought up the name Guiddard. It had struck a bell in his memory and now, looking at the court files, he knew why.

James Guiddard, the man who'd shot and killed Julia's husband, had once faced Harry in court. It had been on a robbery charge, and reading back through the information, Harry was beginning to recall bits and pieces of the case.

Harry felt as if there was a rock sinking to the pit of his stomach. More than a year before Guiddard had killed Officer Warren, he'd set James Guiddard free. It hadn't been by choice. Oh, no, it had been one of those times when Harry had wanted to scream with frustration.

He'd been forced to declare a mistrial because he'd discovered a juror had discussed the trial with a newspaper reporter. Whether the juror actually realized the severity of his actions, or whether he'd done it purposely Harry hadn't known. He had known that many hours of police and courtroom work went down the drain because a tongue had slipped.

Rising from his desk, Harry pulled off his glasses and crossed to stand by the window. His expression pensive, he stared out at the view of the city.

For ten years he'd worked in law. And for six of those he'd been a judge, the one having to make decisions. But it had always been some other family, some other victim, some other loved one who'd felt the final bang of his gavel. He'd always tried his best to be fair and honest. He'd tried to have compassion where it was justified, and toughness where toughness was warranted. He was by no means perfect. He was only a man. And in the case of Guiddard, he'd done the only thing possible.

But would Julia believe that? Was he even going to tell her?

Muttering an oath, he raked a hand through his dark hair. Of course he had to tell her. He couldn't expect to gain her love by keeping secrets from her. Still, he was afraid to consider how she might react to this. It had taken him so long to break through that reserve of hers. And now, just when she was letting down her barriers, he had to dump something like this on her.

God knew he didn't want to do it. He loved her. He wanted so much to bring happiness into her life. He'd been planning on seeing her tonight to tell her just how much he loved her. Now he was going to have to add something else to it. He didn't know how he was going to do it. Damn it, he couldn't even allow himself the luxury of thinking about it. He had to be in court in thirty minutes. With a weary sigh he turned back to his desk.

It was midmorning before Julia's parents left to go back to Kansas. Julia had hated to see them go. She rarely had the chance to spend time with them, and it would have been nice to have talked with her mother about Harry. But they'd been anxious to get back to the farm before dark.

"Mommy, do you have to work now?"

Christopher had followed Julia her into the bedroom. "Not in the work kitchen," she replied. "Now that Grandma and Grandpa have left to go back to the farm, I've got to finish cleaning house. Want to help?"

"Yuk! Housework is for girls."

"Where did you hear that, young man?"

"From Grandpa."

Julia shook her head and laughed to herself. It was wonderful to have her son back home. "There's not much telling what else he put in your head."

She began to straighten the covers on the bed while Christopher made faces in his mother's vanity mirror.

"He taught me how to spit a watermelon seed. That was fun. And he showed me how to play mumblety-peg."

"You're too young to be playing with a knife," Julia said sternly.

"Oh, Grandpa didn't let me. He just showed me. So that when I get older I can play."

"You like to play with Grandpa, don't you?" she asked, as she fluffed the goose-down pillows.

"I like to play with Harry, too. He's going to show me all about marbles. He says some are called cat's-eyes. Ain't that funny?"

Finished with the bed, Julia turned back to her son. "*Isn't* that funny," she corrected. As for Harry, she thought, she would call him this evening and invite him to supper. She knew he'd want to see Christopher, and she could explain why she hadn't shown up in court today.

Christopher left his place at her vanity and started rifling through a box of things Julia's mother had brought her from the farm.

"Grandma cleaned her closet out. She said all this stuff was yours," Christopher said, as Julia picked up the box and moved it over to the bed.

She hadn't gone through it yet. But she could see that some of it was old clothing and a small cedar jewelry box she'd had when she was a child. "It is. And I've got to put it away somewhere."

Julia went to her closet to see if she had room on a shelf there for the box. When she turned to get it, she saw that Christopher had pulled out an old yellowed newspaper.

"Is this my daddy?" he asked, pointing to a picture on the front.

Moving closer, Julia took the paper from him. "Yes. That's your father."

"He was a policeman, wasn't he?"

Julia nodded as she studied the image of Carl. It didn't hurt anymore to look at his photo. She could look back now and remember the pleasant times instead of feeling nothing but bitterness and grief. Falling in love with Harry had done that for her, she realized.

"What does it say? Is that a story about my daddy?"

Julia scanned the column. It was an article written after Carl had been killed during the robbery. She supposed her mother had kept the paper for her. Julia really didn't want it, but she supposed it might be good to keep it for Christopher. When he grew older he might want to know more about his father.

"It just says what a good policeman he was," she told him.

She was about to fold it and put it away when a name caught her eye. Hargrove. Judge Harris T. Hargrove. What was his name doing in an article about Carl? He'd had nothing do with the conviction of James Guiddard.

She slowly read the short paragraph. James Guiddard had apparently had a long list of arrests before the convenience-store robbery in which Officer Warren was fatally shot. At the time of the shooting, Guiddard was free on $50,000 bail on a charge for transporting stolen goods. Bail had been set in Oklahoma County courthouse by Judge Aaron Cornell. Eleven months earlier, Guiddard had been arrested for armed robbery, and breaking and entering. However, the subsequent trial for those crimes was declared a mistrial by Judge Harris T. Hargrove.

Declared a mistrial. Harris T. Hargrove. The words swam before her eyes until they ran together in a blur of shock and confusion.

Her legs felt suddenly weak and she sank onto the bed. What did it mean? A mistrial. Did Harry let Carl's killer go free, too? Just the thought made her ill.

Pressing a hand to her forehead, she closed her eyes and tossed the paper aside.

"Mommy, are you sick or something?"

Julia had forgotten her son was still in the room. She opened her eyes and tried to smile. "No. I'm just tired." She glanced at the newspaper, then back at Christopher. The churning inside her grew even worse. "Why don't you go outside and play?"

"Because it's raining."

Julia looked toward the windows and saw that rain was indeed falling, spattering the panes with great wet drops.

"Well, go check on Josephine. She's missed you while you were in Kansas." She had to have a moment alone. She had to think.

But what was there to think about? she wondered as Christopher left the bedroom. It was all here in black and white. Harry could have put James Guiddard behind bars where he would never have been able to shoot Carl. Instead, he'd allowed the man to go free. Why hadn't he said something? Had he deliberately kept it from her?

This was a nightmare. Maybe she'd wake up and find none of it was true. But no. The pain in her heart was very, very real. And so were the tears beginning to roll down her cheeks....

Harry's day turned out to be longer than he'd expected. By the time he parked his car in front of Julia's house, it was dark and still drizzling rain.

She answered his knock immediately. "Hi," he said, smiling. "I was going to call, but things ran late and I didn't want to take the time."

She stared at him. This was the man she loved, the man she thought she could share her life with. But all that had changed now. Her heart cracked a little as she said, "It doesn't matter. I have nothing to say to you."

Harry frowned in bewilderment. "What?"

"I think you heard me," she said stiffly, willing herself to remain composed.

She started to shut the door in his face, but Harry quickly pushed past her and into the dimly lit living room. She followed him and he turned to face her. "What do you mean you have nothing to say? I thought…last night you left me with the impression that you were going to give me—us—a chance."

She jammed her hands into the pockets of her jeans and looked up at him. "That was before I found out what kind of man you really are."

His brows lifted more with each word she spoke. He could see she was angry, but why was beyond him. It couldn't be connected to the Guiddard case, he thought. He'd only just discovered that himself. "Oh? And what kind of man am I?"

Something inside Julia snapped and her hurt was replaced by anger. "One who has no place in my life!"

She started to move past him, but Harry grabbed hold of her arm. "What are you talking about, Julia? Last night you were so—" He broke off, shaking his head at the anger in her eyes.

"So gullible. Isn't that the word a judge would use?" she asked dryly.

Harry tried to hold on to his temper as he led her toward the couch and grasped both her hands in his. "What are you doing, Julia?'' he asked as he made her sit down with him. "Did you plan this, rehearse this, because you were afraid the next time I saw you I was going to ask you for a commitment?''

Julia made no reply. She looked into his face because there was no place else to look. He'd hurt her. She might as well face it. Face him.

"Look Julia, I don't know what you're all riled up about. But I didn't come here tonight to fight with you.'' he sighed wearily, then relaxed his grip on her hands. "I have something to tell you. And I don't know exactly how to do it.''

Julia swallowed painfully as his thumbs moved softly over the back of her hands. His touch was so sweet, so wonderful. She'd dreamed of giving him her love, of making a family with him. How could she have allowed her feelings to go so far?

"Just answer one thing, Harry. That's all I want. Why did you set Carl's killer free?''

Her question was the last thing he'd expected, and his face paled. "Julia, I—''

"You deliberately kept that from me, didn't you?''

Her voice quivered with pain and Harris wanted more than anything to take her in his arms and soothe it away.

"Because I had no choice, Julia. A juror was caught discussing the case outside the courtroom. No matter what Guiddard had done, he deserved a fair trial, and it was my job to see that he got one. The best way I knew how.''

Gritting her teeth, she jerked her hands away from his. "Then your best wasn't good enough! You let a killer go free! And all this time I'd been talking about Carl, about the way he'd been killed, you said nothing!''

He threw up his hands in despair. "Because I didn't know anything. I had no idea James Guiddard was the one who killed Carl. In fact, I didn't know until this morning when Jim happened to mention it."

"I can't believe that. You couldn't have forgotten."

"Julia, do you think I'm superhuman? I've resided over hundreds of cases since then. How was I supposed to make the connection between James Guiddard and your husband?"

She rammed her fingers through her hair and pressed them tightly against her scalp as if to squeeze out the pain. "I don't know. I don't even suppose it matters anymore," she muttered, closing her eyes.

"What does that mean?"

Julia wondered how long it was going to be before the tears burning in the backs of her eyes surfaced and made a fool of her.

"It means that whatever we had between us is over. I don't want to see you again."

Harry felt as if she'd stabbed him. "Why?"

Her eyes flew open at his question. "Why? You have to ask why? How could I ever expect to have a future with you? How could I forget that you helped kill my husband!"

Harry reached out and shook her by the shoulders. "I didn't help kill anyone!"

"Maybe it eases your conscience to see it that way."

Releasing a frustrated breath, he said, "You're the one having trouble seeing things as they really are. You can't see anything because you're too busy throwing blame at judges, juries, lawyers, anything that has to do with the legal system. Hell, I guess you even blame the country."

Tossing back her hair, she rose from the couch. "Don't be ridiculous," she muttered. "I love this country."

He laughed harshly. "You don't love its laws. And let's face it, Julia, that's what makes the United States so unique and so wonderful."

She whirled back to him. "Do you think it's right that Guiddard was allowed to go free?"

Harry shook his head. "No. But it was the law. And whether those laws are right or wrong, we, I, have to stand by them." He got to his feet, too. "Those laws and those judges you keep blaming are here to protect the innocent. And everyone is innocent until proven guilty—even me."

Tears began to stream down her face. "Do you want to hear something ironic? I was planning to tell you that it no longer mattered to me that you were a judge. I really believed I could put everything behind me and start a life with you."

Harry stepped closer and touched her shoulder. She was trembling, and though he should have been angry at her blind stubbornness, he found himself wanting to pull her into his arms and make love to her.

"You can start a life with me, Julia," he said gently. "All you have to do is let yourself."

How could he say that? Was everything so simple to him, so black and white?

Her eyes were full of pain and confusion as his hands came up to frame her face.

"I love you, Julia. Surely you know that by now. I want you to be my wife. I want to be a father to Chris. I want us to have brothers and sisters for him. We could have a wonderful life together. All you have to do is let it happen."

He loved her. He wanted to marry her. Yesterday Julia would have been thrilled to hear him say those words. But now she was numb with betrayal.

"I thought I loved you, too," she said, her voice deadened with pain.

His eyes narrowed on her pale face. "You thought you loved me? That's a hell of a big difference from knowing!"

"What do you expect from me, Harry? I just learned you contributed to my husband's death! Am I just supposed to forget it?"

His hands dropped to her shoulders, and his fingers bit into her flesh. "I'll tell you what I want, Julia," he said, his eyes flashing angrily. "I want you to quit thinking about your dead husband and start thinking about me!"

She went still. "How could you—"

"That's what this whole thing is about, Julia. It's not who killed Carl. It's the fact that you just don't want to let him go. Hanging on to his ghost means more to you than I do!"

"That's not true!" she burst out, then covered her face with trembling hands. "I knew if I let myself get involved with you that either you or me, or both of us, was going to end up getting hurt," she said, her voice muffled by her fingers and another surge of oncoming tears. "And I'm tired of hurting, Harry."

His fingers eased their grip and slid gently up her throat and into her hair. "Julia, please," he said softly, "if you would only look ahead instead of back you could see us together. You could see how happy we could be."

Sobs began to shake her shoulders and desperately she turned her back to him. "I don't want to see you at all. Ever."

Grimly he started toward the door. Once he reached it, he looked back. She was still crying, her face hidden by a curtain of hair. Pain filled him and he knew now why it hurt to love.

"Maybe you're right about me, Julia," he said huskily. "Maybe I haven't always made the decisions I should have. Maybe someone else should take my place and he can make all the crime go away. No stealing, raping, killing. My God, I'd step down in a minute if that could be so. But I'm a realist, Julia. And the reality is that one man can't make it all go away."

She lifted her head and looked at him through tear-drenched eyes as he went on, "Whether my decisions have been right or wrong, I've at least had the courage to make them. If you ever decide you have the courage to love me, let me know."

Julia watched him walk out the door, the pain in her chest so fierce that she sobbed aloud and flung herself on the couch.

The courage to love him, she thought, as hot tears poured from her heart. Right now she didn't know how she was going to find the courage to survive the night.

Chapter Thirteen

Three days later Julia was in the work kitchen, staring at the wall while she absently stirred a simmering pot of barbecue sauce.

Across the room, Rhonda had taken a break to drink a glass of iced tea and indulge Christopher in a game of guessing riddles.

"Let's see," Rhonda said thoughtfully. "You said it was gray and had a trunk. That's easy. It has to be an elephant."

Christopher giggled loudly. "No, Auntie Rhonda. That's wrong."

"Wrong? I don't believe it. What other kind of animal could be gray and have a trunk?"

"A mouse going on vacation."

Rhonda laughed then gave his tummy a little pinch. "You little stinker. You're too tricky. I'll bet your Grandpa told you that."

He shook his head. "No. Harry told me," he said proudly.

Back at the stove it took everything Julia possessed to keep from groaning aloud. For the past three days all she'd heard from Christopher was Harry this, and Harry that. When was Harry coming?

She knew Christopher loved Harry, and knowing that made Julia feel even more miserable. How was her son going to take it when he found out Harry was never coming back? She dreaded the moment. She'd never wanted Christopher to be hurt because she'd let her heart be led by a man.

She stirred the sauce again, while behind her Christopher and Rhonda continued their game, but she didn't hear what either of them were saying. In fact, Julia was so lost in her dismal thoughts that a few minutes later she didn't hear Rhonda's approach until her friend was already standing right next to her.

"I told Christopher he could go over to Michelle's for an hour or so," Rhonda said.

Julia's glance at Rhonda was vacant. "He can't cross the street by himself. You'll have to call her."

Rhonda rolled her eyes. "I've already helped him cross the street."

"Oh. I didn't realize you'd left the kitchen."

Groaning, Rhonda said, "I'm not surprised. Are you sure you know where you are?"

Julia frowned. "Don't be a smarty. I'm not in the mood for it."

Rhonda snorted. "You're not in the mood for anything except moping. When are you going to do something about it?"

Julia directed her gaze back to the pot of sauce. "Rhonda, we have a small dinner party to prepare for tonight. Now is not the time for you to start badgering me about Harry."

Rhonda leaned a hip against the nearby cabinet and fixed a questioning look on Julia. "So. At least you're admitting the problem is Harry."

Julia continued to stir the sauce even though it didn't need it. "I never denied it was Harry."

Throwing up her hands, Rhonda said, "Julia, I can't understand you. Obviously you love the guy. I've seen the pain on your face since you shut him out of your life. Frankly, I think your thinking has gone completely haywire."

"And what makes you such an authority on love? I don't see you winning any blue ribbons in that department."

"Go ahead," Rhonda said blithely, "be nasty and sarcastic about it. You know you can't hurt me. We've been friends too long for that. Right now I know you're really hurting and I'll be damned if I'm going to stand by and do nothing about it."

Julia turned away from the stove and slumped defeatedly onto a step stool. "I don't know how you can do anything about it when I can't do anything about it myself."

"Bull!" Rhonda snapped before walking away.

Totally surprised by Rhonda's abruptness, Julia watched her cross the room and dump the remainder of her tea into the sink. When Rhonda switched on the radio and started gathering ingredients for yeast dough, Julia knew she wasn't going to launch her tirade after all.

Julia marched over to her. "Bull! What's that supposed to mean?"

Rhonda dumped a small amount of milk into a saucepan. "Just that," Rhonda replied. "The man loves you,

you love him. What more do you want? Everything perfectly wrapped on a silver platter with a written guarantee to go with it?''

"You're being mean.''

"No, I'm being realistic!''

Rhonda huffed angrily and Julia wiped a weary hand across her forehead.

"I have been miserable without Harry," Julia admitted in a small voice. "These past few days everything has been—" She broke off helplessly as Harry's handsome image swam before her eyes. "I didn't know what it was like to love like this, Rhonda. It's as if my world has turned black because he's not going to be with me. Do you know what I mean?''

Rhonda's features softened with understanding. "Unfortunately I do. That's why you have to do something about it, Julia. If you really love him, you can't let anything come between you. Especially something that's really no fault of Harry's.''

Julia sighed. Rhonda was right. These past few days she'd done a lot of thinking. Bitterness had become a way of life with her. She'd thrived on that wasteful emotion for so long that she'd forgotten all about love until Harry had come along. She wanted to fill her heart with Harry's love. With her love for him.

"I've searched my soul, Rhonda, and the only thing I keep coming up with is that I don't want to live the rest of my life without Harry.''

Rhonda suddenly let out a whoop of joy. "Hallelujah! You've finally come to your senses!''

Julia smiled for the first time in days. "I guess I have, haven't I?''

Rhonda grabbed her by the arm. "Hurry. Get in the house and change your clothes. I want you to go see him now. This minute."

"Rhonda! We have a dinner to serve tonight. It's only three hours away and I still have to make that chocolate soufflé."

"Damn, I forgot about the soufflé!" Rhonda said with a snap of her fingers. "Well, at least you can call him. Go on." She shooed Julia toward the door. "Go to the house so you won't have to worry about me listening."

Now that she'd finally made a decision, Julia felt as if her heart had taken wing. Grinning she opened the door. "I don't know why. You're going to ask me everything that was said, anyway."

She could hear Rhonda's laughter following her outside. But once in the house she forgot all about Rhonda's bolstering talk. Her hands began to shake as she searched through the phone directory for the courthouse number. Finally she found it and started to punch out the numbers. She didn't know exactly what she was going to say to him, but she hoped he would still love her enough to listen.

"Wait, Julia!"

Julia gave a start as Rhonda stumbled into the room. She was out of breath and looked frightened.

"What's wrong?"

Rhonda took a gulp of air, then rushed to the television. "I don't know if I heard the radio right or not, but it said that a Judge Hargrove was being held hostage in his courthouse chambers."

Julia was so stunned she could merely stare at Rhonda. Hostage? Harry? No! That couldn't be right.

Fear suddenly ripped through her and set her heart pounding. She shot to her feet and joined Rhonda in front of the television.

The screen had finally come to life, and both women stood stock-still as they watched a live scene of the courthouse surrounded by police and media people.

"Oh, my God! It must be true," Julia whispered, stricken. "Rhonda! It must be true!"

Before Rhonda could say anything Julia ran to the kitchen and grabbed her car keys. "Tell Michelle to keep Christopher with her."

"Where are you going?" Rhonda cried as Julia hurried to the front door.

"I've got to go down there!"

"Are you crazy? You can't do anything. We don't even know what's happening yet."

"I have to go! If something happens to him..." She couldn't bear to finish the sentence. Instead she raced down the steps and out to her car. Julia was in the car and reversing it onto the street before Rhonda could stop her.

By the time she reached the courthouse, Julia was shaking all over. After parking as near to the building as possible, she pushed through the crowd of people that had gathered on the lawn.

"Sorry, ma'am, no one can go in or out of the courthouse," an officer told her when she reached the front entrance of the building.

Julia looked desperately up the long steps leading inside. She was almost tempted to try to rush by the officer before he could stop her.

"You need to let me in there—"

The officer interrupted her. "It's impossible, ma'am. We have a hostage situation inside the building."

"I know! Harry is..." Harry was everything to her! If something happened to him, her very life would be gone, too. It was so simple to see that now.

She grabbed frantically at the officer's sleeve. "Harry is going—I mean, Judge Hargrove is going to be my husband. I have to know he's all right! Please!"

Her words caught the officer's attention and he looked at her more closely. "You know Judge Hargrove?"

"Yes! Now please let me go in! At least tell me what's going on!"

His expression changed to one of sympathy as he watched tears swim in her beautiful gray eyes. "At this moment all we know is that a man somewhere in his mid-fifties is holding a gun on Judge Hargrove—"

Julia drew a sharp breath, and the officer held up his hand and went on, "So far no shots have been fired. The security people are waiting to see if Judge Hargrove can talk the man into giving up the gun before they make any kind of move."

"But why?" she whispered fearfully. "Why Harry? Why would anyone want to hurt him?"

He shrugged. "Who knows about some of these kooks? They get it in their heads that the law has wronged them, and they usually target someone at the top to get their revenge."

Revenge. It was such an ugly word. Why would anyone want to get revenge against Harry? He only wanted to help people.

But right behind that thought came the realization that Julia had been guilty of her own sort of revenge. And it had been so wrongly directed at Harry....

Oh, dear God, she silently prayed, don't take Harry from me now. Don't let it be too late for me to tell him how wrong I've been, how much I love him.

The minutes ticked into an hour. An hour passed into two. The sun began to sink in the west and twilight settled over the courthouse lawn.

Julia, who'd been agitatedly pacing the lawn, finally wore herself out and now simply stood staring up at the light filtering through the windows of Harry's office. The blinds were pulled, making it impossible to see what was going on in the room.

"Are you all right, ma'am?"

She looked around to see the same young officer she'd spoken to earlier. She nodded grimly. "I'd just like to know what's going on in there," she said.

"Wouldn't we all."

She looked back at the windows. "I first met Harry in that room," she said, her voice pensive. "He was eating a peanut-butter-and-jelly sandwich. And I thought he was gorgeous."

The officer patted her shoulder as tears burned her eyes. "The gunman hasn't hurt him yet. That's a good sign. If something doesn't break soon the SWAT team will move in."

Inside the courthouse Harry sat behind his desk, eyeing the tormented gunman. He was a small man with a leathery face and blue eyes that darted constantly around the room.

"What do you say we have a cup of coffee?" Harry suggested. "We've been sitting here a long time. I've got a coffeepot right over there."

The man's eyes darted to the coffeepot then back to Harry. "Don't you move! You move and I'll shoot you." The pistol wavered as he pointed it at Harry's chest.

Harry rubbed a tired hand over his face and through his hair. "You're not going to shoot me. We've been sitting here for two hours and you haven't shot me yet."

"I will! If you try anything I'll put a hole in you."

His patience stretched to the limit, Harry propped his chin on his fist. "Then go ahead and do it. I don't care if you do."

The gunman stared at Harry. "You're lyin'."

"No, I'm not. I've decided this job is too much hell. It's caused me to lose the woman I love. So you see, I don't have much to look forward to, anyway."

"You ain't gonna make me believe that. Women like you big-shot guys."

Harry smiled faintly. Some women might. But not Julia. He'd never known a woman like her. Stubborn, opinionated, passionate. He couldn't stop thinking about her even now. Especially now. "I'm not a big shot. There're lots of judges with more clout than me."

The gunman squinted as he took another look at his captive. "Don't believe that, neither."

Leaning back in his chair, Harry crossed his arms over his chest. "Well, it's true. I'm only an associate district judge. There's a district judge over me. Then there's supreme court judges. They all have much more say-so than I do."

The little man shook his head. "They don't do nothin'. You're the one I'm always readin' about in the papers. You're the one who's always sendin' all those crooks and killers to jail."

"When the crime warrants it I do, but—"

"That's why I know you can help me. You can do somethin' about that mean son of a—"

"I told you there's no way I can help you, or your daughter, unless she'll come forward and press charges against her husband. If you'll put that gun down so we can really talk, I'll tell you the ways I might be able to help."

The gun lowered, but the barrel was still directed at Harry. "I told the police and the lawyers that he was dealin' drugs," the man went on. "But they said they had to have proof, evidence. Hellfire! What do they need? A dead body? Do they need to see me or my daughter dead before they can do anything about it?"

"No. If he's physically abusing your daughter and she can prove it . . ." Harry's words trailed off as he spotted Jim slipping through the door leading from Edith's office. He didn't know what the security guard had in mind, but he knew he had to act as normally as possible and keep the gunman distracted. "The law will be able to put him away," he finished.

"She's scared. Don't you know that? He said he'd kill her if she talked to the police."

"And what is he going to do if he finds out you're here talking to me?" Jim was creeping closer, but so far the little man was completely unaware that someone was behind him. Harry continued. "What if he hurts her while you're sitting here wasting time?"

The determination on the little man's face wavered, and Harry silently prayed he was getting through to him.

"Put down the gun and call her. You need to make sure she's all right. If he's there hurting her, we'll send a squad car to help."

The man's eyes went from Harry to the telephone then back to Harry.

"You're tryin' to trick me."

Harry shook his head, then picked up the telephone and held it out. "What's more important? Holding that gun on me or making sure your daughter is safe?"

Tense seconds ticked slowly by before the man finally put the gun down on the desk and reached for the telephone.

At that moment Jim made a lunge for the man while Harry snatched up the pistol.

Jim struggled with the little man for only a moment before he was able to fasten handcuffs on him.

"You're just like the rest of them," the man angrily spat at Harry.

Harry put the gun safely away and went around the desk. "No. I'm not like the rest of them. I promised to help and I will." He patted the man's shoulder, then looked up at Jim. "Thanks, Jim. If you ever quit your job, I'm going to be in big trouble."

The security guard smiled proudly at the praise. "You're welcome, Judge. Now what do I do with this fella?"

"Let me call his daughter. We'll do something about all of this later."

The news that it was all over leaked to the crowd before Harry appeared on the steps of the courthouse. Julia was weeping with relief as she watched anxious TV and newspaper reporters rush to get a statement from him.

"Was it someone you'd convicted, Judge?" one asked.

"No. I'd never seen him before."

"Was he a mental patient?"

Grimacing, Harry tried to move forward through the surging crowds. "No. The man was not a mental patient. He was just a person in trouble."

"Judge, at any time did you think the man would shoot you?" a female reporter asked, jamming a microphone in his face.

"If you're asking if I feared for my life, the answer is no." Oddly enough, facing the barrel of a pistol hadn't been nearly as daunting to Harris as having to face his life without Julia in it.

At the bottom of the steps Julia struggled to get through the crowd and catch Harry's attention.

"Harry! Harry!"

He heard her voice first, then caught sight of her red hair. She was here! Waiting for him! His weary heart suddenly burst with happiness.

Breaking free of the press, he rushed to meet her. "Julia!"

She stumbled and nearly fell as he reached out and swept her into his arms. "You're here. You're really here," he said, his voice raw with emotion.

Julia clung to him tightly. Nothing had ever felt as good as touching him, having him safe. "Oh, Harry! Thank God you're all right."

"I am now that you're here," he said with a groan. "I've missed you so!"

Oblivious to the people around them, Julia lifted her face to his. "I love you, Harry," she whispered fervently. "Can you forgive me for being so blind?"

Joy swept across his face. "Forgive you? My darling, I'm going to marry you. As quickly as possible."

Tears of happiness blurred her eyes as she smiled up at him. "Is it all right for a judge to be kissed on the courthouse lawn?"

Laughing, Harry bent his head and proceeded to show her just how right it was.

* * * * *

This is the season of giving, and Silhouette proudly offers you its sixth annual Christmas collection.

SILHOUETTE

Christmas Stories

1991

Experience the joys of a holiday romance and treasure these heartwarming stories by four award-winning Silhouette authors:

Phyllis Halldorson—"A Memorable Noel"
Peggy Webb—"I Heard the Rabbits Singing"
Naomi Horton—"Dreaming of Angels"
Heather Graham Pozzessere—"The Christmas Bride"

Discover this yuletide celebration—sit back and enjoy Silhouette's Christmas gift of love.

SILHOUETTE CHRISTMAS STORIES 1991 is available in December at your favorite retail outlet, or order your copy now by sending your name, address, zip or postal code, along with a check or money order for $4.99 (please do not send cash), plus 75¢ postage and handling ($1.00 in Canada), payable to Silhouette Books, to:

In the U.S.
3010 Walden Ave.
P.O. Box 1396
Buffalo, NY 14269-1396

In Canada
P.O. Box 609
Fort Erie, Ontario
L2A 5X3

Please specify book title with your order.
Canadian residents add applicable federal and provincial taxes.

SX91-2

WRITTEN IN THE STARS

WHEN A CAPRICORN MAN MEETS A GEMINI WOMAN...

Wealthy dairy farmer Adam Challow's no-nonsense approach to life wavered when he met the enticing Gemini beauty, Donna Calvert. The normally steadfast Capricorn didn't want to trust his feelings, but Donna was simply irresistible! Joan Smith's FOR RICHER, FOR POORER is coming this January from Silhouette Romance. After all, it's WRITTEN IN THE STARS!

Silhouette Romance

LONG, TALL TEXANS

DONAVAN
Diana Palmer

Diana Palmer's bestselling LONG, TALL TEXANS series continues with DONAVAN....

From the moment elegant Fay York walked into the bar on the wrong side of town, rugged Texan Donavan Langley knew she was trouble. But the lovely young innocent awoke a tenderness in him that he'd never known...and a desire to make her a proposal she couldn't refuse....

Don't miss DONAVAN by Diana Palmer, the ninth book in her LONG, TALL TEXANS series. Coming in January...only from Silhouette Romance.

LTT192

YOU'VE ASKED FOR IT, YOU'VE GOT IT!

MAN OF THE MONTH: 1992

ONLY FROM
SILHOUETTE® *Desire™*

You just couldn't get enough of them, those sexy men from Silhouette Desire—twelve sinfully sexy, delightfully devilish heroes. Some will make you sweat, some will make you sigh . . . but every long, lean one of them will have you swooning. So here they are, men we couldn't resist bringing to you for one more year. . . .

A KNIGHT IN TARNISHED ARMOR
by Ann Major in January

THE BLACK SHEEP
by Laura Leone in February

THE CASE OF THE MESMERIZING BOSS
by Diana Palmer in March

DREAM MENDER
by Sheryl Woods in April

WHERE THERE IS LOVE
by Annette Broadrick in May

BEST MAN FOR THE JOB
by Dixie Browning in June

Don't let these men get away! *Man of the Month,* only in Silhouette Desire.

Take 4 bestselling love stories FREE
Plus get a FREE surprise gift!

NORA ROBERTS

Love has a language all its own, and for centuries, flowers have symbolized love's finest expression. Discover the language of flowers—and love—in this romantic collection of 48 favorite books by bestselling author Nora Roberts.

Starting in February 1992, two titles will be available each month at your favorite retail outlet.

In February, look for:

Irish Thoroughbred, Volume #1
The Law Is A Lady, Volume #2

Collect all 48 titles and become fluent in the Language of Love.

LOL192

THE LANGUAGE of LOVE